small acts of sex and electricity

unbridled books

small acts of sex and electricity

lise haines

Unbridled Books
Denver, Colorado

Library of Congress Cataloging-in-Publication Data
Haines, Lise.
Small acts of sex and electricity / Lise Haines.
p. cm.
ISBN-13: 978-1-932961-27-0
ISBN-10: 1-932961-27-5
1. Female friendship—Fiction. 2. Marriage—Fiction. 3. Women—Family
relationships—Fiction. 4. Psychological fiction. 5. Domestic fiction. I. Title.
PS3608.A545S63 2006
813'.6–dc22   2006015449

1   3   5   7   9   10   8   6   4   2

Book Design by SH•CV

First Printing

to Sienna, Charis and Ben

small acts of sex and electricity

one

I found Mike passed out on the master bed, curled on his side, the covers down around the floor. Maybe he had kicked them off. Sometimes he and Jane slept that way. There was a tiny pool of moisture where the tip of his penis touched the bedding, a dimple at the base of his spine. He had a very long back. Spider veins just below his ankles. Mike was losing hair in a circle at the back of his head, in the same spot where a man of God shaves his skull.

To get to him, I had inched down the hall, past the clock room where their daughters, Livvy and Mona, slept. Locking the door behind me in case they got up, I stood by the blue dust ruffle. I was supposed to wake Mike and tell him that Jane, his wife, my oldest friend, had just left him. She had driven off in Franny's Jaguar.

I wondered how Mike would talk with Livvy and Mona. I wasn't sure what I'd say. Livvy, the older girl, was the one who worried me. No one would be awake for hours.

Mike's voice bubbled up but made no sense. Refined alcohol came with each of his exhalations, the occasional choked snore. His face animated and relaxed. I wanted to be with Mike in that raw, unkempt state. But I knew how many cables there are in the elevator shafts of the Empire State Building and how long it takes for a body to hit the sidewalk if you jump from the roof. And I was aware, as I stood by the side of the bed, that I could screw up in so many ways, up or down. It was hard to know where Mike would land if he jumped.

To get my head on the pillow, I nudged him a little. He knew how to breathe from his diaphragm even in his sleep. I touched the spot over his missing appendix, surprised that he didn't wake, and curled into his back. Then froze. I heard a boat move through the water, close to the house.

I made a ring out of my left thumb and forefinger and fitted it around his penis. He stiffened and angled and his hips moved in what appeared to be deep REM sleep. His back twitched a little. I waited, as if a horn or bell would go off, signaling the start of my trade with Jane.

I slipped my hand away and put it under my ribs to feel my irregular heartbeat. I thought about basic survival, considered social membranes, tried to review one of those rules that keep people in check. The house sounded like an engine cooling. If I just shut my eyes for one minute, I'd be able to straighten things out. But it was too easy to siphon off his REM. I hadn't slept in days and I guess I'd exhausted all thoughts of survival.

. . . . . .

When Jane left Mike, she took her grandmother's Jaguar. A coffee-brown machine with a mocha interior and custom tortoiseshell trim along the dash and armrests. It was built in 1965 and I had spent summers from the time I was eight sticking to its leather seats, flipping the ashtray covers open and shut with Jane. Her grandmother, Franny, ground forty years of Chanel No. 5 into the ball of the stick shift. She was big on original ownership. But now Franny was dead and her family still hadn't decided what they'd do with the car.

Jane had come down to the kitchen at four that morning. I was up because I never slept at Franny's house. But Jane typically woke in the afternoon when she drank hard. So I didn't understand why she was standing there, fully dressed, as if she wanted to get an early start.

She had that rehashed Audrey Hepburn look: blue summer dress, thin belt, sandals fastened with leather straps. She filled the pot and scooped level measures of coffee into the machine, sat down at the table across from me. She looked as if she were going to say something, stopped, then told me Mike and the girls were still asleep, as if I needed reassurance about this. I listened to the Pacific as it hit the pilings, and I looked at Jane's lipstick, not sure why she'd bothered. Her eyelashes—they would have disappeared if it weren't for the mascara.

—You do something to your hair? I asked.

It appeared to be hacked at, not cut. I didn't think it had been like that earlier in the evening.

—Sort of.

I began to glide the salt and pepper shakers across the table, waiting for her to continue. Figure eights, in and out of the light from the overhead spot. Jane had once been offered a job as an eye model with a good New York agency. You could magnify those eyes until you were looking down at Earth. They were that blue. It's a bad form of envy to want someone else's face. I tipped my head to one side to get the full effect of her butchered hair.

—You use Mona's scissors?

She stopped the movement of the salt but couldn't quite reach the hand with the pepper.

—In a fair world you'd have kids, Mattie.

Her daughters were asleep in the clock room. Mona was four then, Livvy fourteen.

—I'm too tired for the fair-world conversation, I said.

—You can't expect to . . . no, I don't mean that. I don't know how long you plan on . . .

I had that queasiness I get when a salesman leans against my buzzer.

—I'm only thirty-five and I didn't sleep last night, Jane.

—Humor me with a what-if.

—I should have gotten up to read.

—You want a whole life, don't you? she asked.

—Define whole life.

—Marriage . . .

I saw the strain, the need to talk. I knew it wasn't about

my sense of family. Whatever it was, I couldn't respond. In that way you imagine you have influence over events, I've punished myself for that moment.

—You didn't sign me up for an on-line dating service, did you? Because I've looked at those men.

She began to fold and unfold one of the linen napkins left on the table.

—I know this is about Franny. . . . I open the towel cabinet and it's like she's standing there, waiting for me to make some right decision, I said.

—About the towels?

—Which ones should go to the women's shelter because the edges haven't frayed, which ones to the Salvation Army. . . .

—She'd appreciate what you're doing. I appreciate it. More than you know.

Periodically, Jane used to send me snaps taken at their home outside Boston. Mona wore reindeer antlers, or rabbit ears, sat by giant jack-o'-lanterns. Livvy was the one with her back to the camera, walking out of the frame, her hair blue or green, the back of her jacket pounded with studs that formed messages I couldn't read. I had a soft spot for Livvy. Mike was the lens. It was his job to catch and measure light, to wait for conditions. I watched what he did to get a picture. He tugged on something emotional, sometimes the thing he couldn't state. Maybe he'd frame a tiny gas station sign in one corner of an image that said exactly what he couldn't express with the large people in the foreground. But if your eye was sharp and you knew how to read backwards or thought to hold it up to a mirror, it was all there. I looked for Mike's face in those photographs—sometimes Jane would nail him. The dark moods and then a shot that would make me think *A Hard Day's Night,* the antic self. But it was mostly Jane, and sometimes I had the sense, looking at her, that she understood something I was going through at the time. Maybe it was a mind trick, but that was what I thought Jane did, made people feel no one else fully understood them. I said that to Mike one time, and he laughed. Later he said maybe I was right.

—You look like you're going to the store, I said to Jane.

Up the road, Von's grocery was open twenty-four hours. That was the place to order a sheet cake if you had to, the red frosting dyed your tongue red, the blue blue. You could get arugula at Von's, deodorant, hybrid chickens.

—I've never said this to you, maybe because we were both a little drunk at the time, but I told Mike once, if anything happened to me, he should marry you.

—You're upsetting my stomach, I said.

I got busy wiping down the edges of the sink, my face heated.

—He brought it up the next morning when we were perfectly sober. He asked me if I had been serious. I said: Yes. And he said . . . well, he said a lot of things.

I couldn't tell if she was trying to peel my layers or if she had done that already and was holding me up to the light. I watched her remove the coffee pot halfway into its drip. Coffee spit against the hot plate, a trickle slipped onto the counter and pooled. She threw her napkin down to soak it up.

At moments like that I pictured Franny smoking a cigarette close to the window so the fumes wouldn't fill the house, encouraging me to speak up. And when that didn't work, she would offer to play a round of Chinese Checkers with me.

I couldn't get what Jane was up to.

—I'm not sure why I deserve this conversation . . . but can we wait until my head clears? I didn't even close my eyes last night, no flying dreams, no psycho nightmares of my mother, just the clock room echoing through the floor. I hope you plan on selling the clocks.

—You're veering off, she said.

—Veering off what? I don't want to think about anything happening to you, okay?

—But that's irrational.

—Why don't we talk about the vases?

Jane turned on the radio. The way she leaned into the counter, the outfit, she was imitating Franny, that force of gravity that had me pinned.

A polka came on. When that was over, the day's headlines. An express truck had blown up in the Midwest. The driver's remains scattered hundreds of feet. And this side note: *Many letters had survived.*

—I bet they'll put them in plastic sleeves and Forensics will impound them, I said.

—What?

—The letters.

—I wasn't listening, she said.

—They blew up an express truck.

I was picturing a team of FBI guys in an airplane hanger somewhere in the dessert, reconstructing the truck, the man. . . .

But she was someplace else, going through the drawer now where Franny used to keep the cooking thermometer, the small strainers and matches. Jane took out some papers and set them down on the table. I looked at the girls' medical insurance cards, Livvy's was on top. Her middle name was my proper first name: Madeleine. There were airline tickets, numbers with the Boston 617 area code, a birth certificate that looked to be Mona's. I didn't know people carried their kids' birth records on trips.

Then she glanced around as if she had forgotten something, took a half gallon of milk out of the fridge, and left the kitchen.

—We're running low on Kleenex, I called.

I followed her into the garage with my cup, trying to think of other items we needed.

Jane propped the milk carton on the front seat. I saw a couple of Franny's old blue suitcases in the back. Jane yanked on the rope attached to the bottom of the garage door and released it upward along its track. Then she got in on the driver's side.

—Where the hell are you going?

Outside, a thick marine layer. From up in the foothills the kind of condensation that looks like cream sitting in a dish.

—I'll get money to you, she said.

—I'm not charging a fee. I told you that.

She turned the engine over. I stood by the driver's side, looking at her face. I thought of those movies set to Philip Glass music: clouds in time lapse, traffic sped up, flowers that open faster than I can sneeze.

—Okay, what if. What if you go crazy and don't come back? I said, trying to be funny.

She took a long draw of the milk and wedged the carton between her legs. The hibiscus around the garage hadn't opened yet. The petals were twisted round their stamens like pink tissue paper. Maybe if I stood there long enough they'd uncoil.

—But that's the point. I could live as free and easy as . . . as you.

—Why are you so pissed at me? Look, my old boss might have a job coming up. I told you that. I need to get back to Chicago.

She drank some more. Her eyes welled.

—Is Mike planning to watch the girls? So I can sort through things . . .

—You don't get it, she said.

—He doesn't know?

Jane had me standing out in the alley behind Franny's house, freezing to death in a shortie nightgown because someone had to be her audience and she wanted to hit the road early. She sat there idling in first, and was, I think, prepared to drive to God-knows-where.

—You tell him.

—Get out of the car and talk.

—You're getting a good trade. . . . What's the name of that TV show? she asked.

—What TV show?

—Where the two friends switch places, she said.

—You mean, houses?

—Us. I mean us, everything. Mike, the girls. You know, like a kit-home. Easy to assemble.

—Easy to what?

—You'll be more efficient than me.

—More efficient at *your* life? That's bizarre. . . .

She put the car in reverse and I reached for her door handle. But she suddenly pulled out of the garage and backed straight into a hedge. The engine cut out and she pushed her chopped hair away from her face, leaned her forehead into her palm, on a backwards reel.

—At least turn your lights on.

Jane straightened up and started the car again.

—Go back inside, she said.

—You want me to drive? I just have to run in and get a couple of things.

Her face made me think of an underground nuclear test. The car jerked forward and the rear bumper stripped a thousand tiny leaves from the shrubs. I should have grabbed my lavender sweater the minute I saw the suitcases.

Jane began to navigate the narrow lane. She swerved to avoid the garbage cans. There were liquor bottles by the cans, boxes from new household appliances, and broken Styrofoam beach items. I hoped she'd hit a garbage can. I needed time to stall her. I looked at her outfit again.

—Are you going to meet some guy?

I had shouted it to be heard above the waves. I think her foot slipped off the clutch at that point, which killed the engine again. She turned around, briefly. I noticed her lipstick. She yelled:

—Full Stop!

I watched her accelerate as if she was kicking off from the side of a pool, but she didn't circle at the other end. She had gotten her impulse thing from her father and it hit in cycles like El Niño. I felt certain she wouldn't abandon the girls, that she'd quickly send for them, get Mike to drive them to her. She had to. I tried to follow the car but my feet were being eaten up by the gravel in the alley. I'm not sure if she could hear me anymore. I knew the carton of milk was sweating into her dress. I worried that it might tip forward, that the distraction could cause an accident.

Finally Jane switched her lights on, but all I could see were two red circles floating in white air. I imagined the car was lined up with the gate's sensors. The security gate opened and the taillights moved across the tar road. She turned right, away from the beach.

I pictured a sudden collision, her legs squeezing together spasmodically. Milk like sex, soaking her skirt, the leather bench seat, working its way into crevices, plans.

—Come on, I said, as if Jane were still there, standing next to me, thinking of the girls' breakfast, wondering if she had enough cereal in the house.

The fog failed to put out my anger. If she wanted to trade, I had very different things to put on the table. She lived in a six-bedroom home outside Boston with a studio above the garage. I lived in a remodeled and largely reduced loft space in Chicago, two bedrooms, one of them only ten by ten, one bath, the porches had been an add-on, making use of the framework of the old elevator shafts. A courtyard in the center of the building. Jane was a set designer for large regional theaters. I appraised fine arts and antiques. She worked part time. I worked chronically. But she had returned to the same guy each night, the same conversations, the habit of sleeping on one side of the bed or the other, listening for their girls in the dark. Forms of possession I didn't know.

I did have good friends in Chicago. I went to a fitness center and had started a kickboxing class. I liked to shoot pool, joined a team once, which nudged me to get a monogrammed cue and a special pair of gloves for a decent grip, small cubes of blue chalk. I tried a birding group. I was a collector. I had an investment in antique neon signs and the works of small-scale tube-benders. Sometimes old neon came through the auction house. Sometimes I went out on the road to find it. One of my signs read: *Watch for Signs*. I had them mounted on the walls of the loft and they advertised *The Alpine Motel* and *Texa* gas and *Night Stop,* which probably had something to do with trains or buses or stopping something you were up to in the middle of the night. I never imagined I'd have large holdings. But how can you know?

I believe Lois, my mother, had communicated to me largely through signs when I was a child. She had a beautiful hand and sometimes she doodled a picture of my face and then tacked it on the bathroom mirror along with many reminders, aphorisms, and general warnings. She left one kind of note if she were up drinking in the middle of the night: the scrawl tighter, loopier, many words underlined and capitalized. And another kind of message if she came in fresh from sailing and the boat had placed well in a race. Sometimes she had an expansiveness that brought her into the moment. She bought fresh shelving paper for the kitchen or stopped at the drugstore for cigarettes, found me new dot-to-dot books, and these things she communicated directly, though the shelves went unlined.

But for all that education, I couldn't decipher Jane's signs that morning. I left the garage door up, afraid the automatic opener would stir the house.

I imagined she had reached Highway 101 by then and was traveling north. Like Franny, Jane didn't like the congestion of LA, the heat of San Diego, the enterprise of Mexico. North would take her past Von's, the bird refuge, the zoo, and then, I imagined, she'd hit the switch to put the top up on the Jaguar, determined to make it to the Bay Area without a stop. Of course she'd remember you can't put the top up at freeway speeds. So she'd pull onto the shoulder and discover that the mechanism was broken, the top frozen in its housing: one of those repairs Franny had left undone.

If the marine layer burned off, we had planned to spend the morning tracking the girls from the lower deck of the house. Mona had talked about using an inner tube, which would mean one of us joining her. In the afternoon Jane and I would have chipped away at Franny's things, probably the vases, while the girls entertained themselves. Instead she had driven into a place where the signs seemed to be directing her to unlimited freedom, the tubing on the neon in good shape, no krypton leaks.

I walked through the oil stains on the concrete slab of the garage and left prints on the white linoleum. Heading upstairs, I was aware of the ocean caught in the panes of the French doors, the light. I went into Franny's bedroom, and that was when I got into bed with Mike, and wrapped into sleep with him.

Before that morning, I had thought that certain feelings were invisible and stayed that way, that I could tunnel under and live off bomb-shelter air indefinitely. I hadn't told anyone that I was in love with Mike. Jane and I had met him when we were in college. And then of course they became a couple and so on.

Over the years, I had sometimes found myself sleeping with men who reminded me of Mike. Maybe they loved horse racing, or felt uncomfortable in small rooms, or liked to fix things, or empathized too much, or maybe they just didn't mind my storytelling, and even encouraged it. But I never held on to those men, never introduced them around or took them to familiar restaurants. Mostly they came through my loft in Chicago, looking for towels, razor blades, toast with preserves, and they didn't understand that I was sleeping with someone else, sleeping right through them. They were small acts. Their bodies changed, they softened, and then a round of intense muscle building. The way they fixed on me, that changed too. And when I put my reading glasses on, they distorted entirely and became guys with names I couldn't always remember.

Except for this man a couple of years ago, who pried open one of my eyelids, midact, and asked: *Who am I?* I thought that sex was jarring a metaphysical pin loose. I untangled myself and threw the lubricant back into the bedside table drawer. He accused me of having someone else on my brain, he could feel it. His old girlfriend: she had had someone else on the brain. *I'm disappointed,* he said. It was one of those moments when a man thinks he can put on your father's jacket and parade around. *I'm disappointed in you.* He got up and found his clothes in a heap and left. It was raining, which almost added a note of tragedy to his departure. I watched him from my window. He was drenched when he hailed a taxi.

two

I don't get many clear messages about the future. No crawls at the bottom of my mental screen. I would make a terrible oracle. But sometimes I know things. I knew when Franny was hit by the train. Well, I didn't know that it was a train that took her out, but I knew she was out of life. And when you get that kind of sporadic but intense signal, it's hard to understand how you can miss the obvious things. I missed things with Jane. I should have seen she would take off.

Two weeks before she drove away in the Jaguar, she had phoned me in Chicago. She asked if I'd go through the estate with her. We had lost Franny six months earlier, in the winter, so I had already gone out to California for the funeral. When Jane called, I was getting ready for an off-hours interview, hoping to pick up a gig in an auction house. Afterwards, I had plans to meet friends at a pub. I had been out of work for a while. It was a particularly bad time to make a second trip.

—You're it, she said, as if we were playing a child's game.

—I know a great appraiser in LA: Tony. Tony has four

brothers and they're all appraisers and they'd probably all come up to the house just to see it and . . .

—Things will go quickly, she said.

—I guess anything's possible, but . . .

—I don't want five guys named Tony.

—No, they're . . . I know plenty of others. Some of the best.

—But that's what *you* do, you go through stuff. You're an expert.

I didn't say: *That's like assuming you're willing to mutilate yourself because you sell knives for a living.*

Jane knew I didn't want to be the one to break up Franny's house. It had always been my catch basin, safe landing. Jane's relationship with her grandmother had been held together by friction, and though no one ever said this, though no one fully implied it, Jane was blood and I was stray. And this created a particular sense of order.

I urged someone who would know West Coast values. Then I stood in the middle of my loft in Chicago, held the receiver against my ribs and with one hand hoisted a window open for air. The huge, original frames had been hauled up on a winch and set in place when it had been a button factory. They rode to the top with ease. I looked at the rain hitting my sill, the way it sprinkled the black skirt I wore and the hardwood floor, the spray red from the tail-lights going by. The rush-hour traffic headed from the Loop, the cab late. I put the tiny holes of the receiver to my ear again, looked at the unlit neon signs mounted on my walls. All she wanted was a week of my time.

—You still on the line? she asked.

—Sure.

—Mike and the girls will be there.

I was getting soaked.

—We can do a farewell party to the old place and you can drive the Jaguar while you're out. . . .

I knew that one of Franny's neighbors went over to the house weekly to start the motor and inspect the radiator fins flaking off in the salt air. I had always liked that car, and hoped Franny had had a rash moment and left it to me.

From my door-sized windows, I saw the taxi drive up and back, apparently struggling to find my address. But I'd never be able to change and get to the interview in time.

—This will probably be the last chance to be at Franny's. Nan wants to rent it out until it sells.

No one liked Nan.

—You have to get the art out first, I said.

—That's why we need you, to tell us that kind of thing. Did I say Mona asked about you? And Livvy. I think she'd like your company right now.

I doubted she had asked for me.

—Just for a weekend, to get you started, I said. Three days. Four at the most.

—I found a pretty good ticket online. But you'll have to show a medical illness to back out. No refunds.

A few days later, at O'Hare, I ate a green banana, cottage cheese, and two rubbery eggs from a vending machine before the plane boarded. But I had some of my father's genes, so I couldn't make myself sick.

．．．．．．

When I arrived at the Santa Barbara Airport, I chose a subcompact rental. Jane had offered to pick me up, but you have to have your own car in Southern California or you quickly become a dependent. I felt uneasy as I loaded my bags, and I decided to hold off going straight to the house.

Instead I took a detour to Mountain Drive, up in the foothills. I pulled over on a narrow turnout where I could see the city, the cemetery, a large avocado orchard, the marine layer sitting on the beach, the unlimited sky. The chaparral grows up the steep embankment, castor bean digs in everywhere. I thought of times I had spent with Jane: the joint passed across someone's hot tub, the temperature gauge dropped back into the water. Ease, or something that once felt like ease.

I put the hand brake on and listened to the radio, wondered if I could put the battery at risk that way and stall out there permanently. When that didn't happen, I went down the hill and drove through the grounds of the Miramar Hotel, past the tennis courts and swimming pools we used to invade. The roofs of the Miramar were still that insane blue, like an advertisement without words: neon poured into shingles. *Here. Stay here.* The restaurant train car had a new seating area outside with white canvas umbrellas. People were lined up, waiting for tables. I circled round and turned onto San Ysidro Road, past the craftsman-style church. Jacaranda blossoms parachuted along the railroad ties and drifted over to the beach. It made me laugh to see the small purple flowers descend through the air, as if a drama had been saved up to greet me. I punched in the code to the gate and drove through. Then I sat for a while, my car in idle, taking in salt air like an overload of memory. Each summer I'd almost forget what that was like, an intrusion of ocean sound that builds and tears down other sounds until it disappears entirely.

I parked behind the garage. It was the only house that still had one. Years ago the buildings had been spaced apart and there had been some open parking. But all the additions, the desire to cram more in, had pulled them together like row houses. I unloaded the car.

Jane answered the door that day. She seemed confused by my presence, though we had gone over our flight schedules together two nights before. She was thinner than the last time I had seen her, her hair pinned back with tiny butterfly clips, several of which had come loose, as if they were trying to get away from her head. She stepped back into the hall and caught her foot on the cord of a belly board leaning by the door.

—Goddamn it.

Mike stood in the middle of the living room, knee-deep in luggage. He was bare except for his khaki shorts and a pair of battered flip-flops. He smiled when he saw me staring at him. Jane untangled herself. She kissed me on the mouth. I heard the girls upstairs. Mike took my two bags, kissed my mouth as well, and threw on a t-shirt. Jane asked about my flight and if I were thirsty.

—I wouldn't mind a drink.

Mike put his arm around my waist.

—You're insane for doing this, he said.

—That's me.

—How was the flight? Jane asked a second time.

—Direct, I said.

—And the most interesting person you've spoken with in the last twenty-four hours? Mike asked.

—The Hertz rental agent?

—The next twenty-four will improve, he said.

—The hotel's been purchased by foreign investors. They're going to do a major remodel, make it more of a resort, Jane said.

—Sorry to hear it, I said.

As if she were coming out of a stupor, Jane suddenly offered me something to drink again. But shortly after I said yes, I was thirsty, she looked around, as if she had forgotten something, and then dropped onto the couch. My patience felt like a third suitcase I couldn't put down. Mike made me a Campari and soda. When I think back on that afternoon, I realize they were like two people with broken whisper phones in a science exhibit. They barely made eye contact with one another.

Finally Jane went off to the kitchen and Mike pushed a handful of dolls in various states of undress to one end of the couch so we could sit.

—You okay? he asked.

—I keep expecting Franny to walk through a door. Mike rubbed my shoulders a little.

—You think the foreigners will leave the blue roofs alone?

—Not a chance, I said.

When Jane returned, I dealt with the topic I imagined she and Mike were avoiding or polarized by.

—I'll help you work out a rough plan, I said, breaking the skin on the silence.

Jane flinched. Franny's estate was sizable. She'd been an avid collector of fine and decorative arts. There were the collections of small objects from Africa, Greece, and Egypt; tribal masks; leather-bound books; Moroccan and Chinese rugs. A shelf of skulls: bobcat, hummingbird, pelican. Steel molds once used in making balloons were mounted on marble bases. On the coffee table, a red carnival-glass dish was filled with black wooden spools. And the Louis XIV table. Franny had impressed its existence upon Jane and her sister, Nan, and me each time we had flown into the living room instead of walking. I noted the photograph of Franny that had been framed for the funeral. She looked like one of those Avedon models from the '50s.

—I don't mean anything too detailed. I just need to get an idea of which items will be held out for the family. You can think about what you'd like an exact appraisal on—I'll help you with that. And if you hope to sell by the piece or the lot. But we'll get there, I said, opening my briefcase. I felt like a realtor or mortician giving a pitch. I don't think they understood what it meant to settle an estate, especially one like Franny's. The time for each appraisal, lining up buyers. And things tended to change daily where several interests were involved: the items Jane and Nan would fight over. I knew Jane would hand me the phone, expecting me to settle things between them.

I took a half-dozen yellow rule-lined pads and a box of pens from my case and set them in the middle of the coffee table so they would have them when they were ready.

—You brought office supplies from Chicago? Jane laughed. I struggled with the shrink-wrap covering the tablets. Seeing me grow flustered, she smoothed my hair as if it were flying about from static electricity. Mike gave me a sympathetic look.

It was a cool morning, but a couple of swimmers were out in the short waves now. For the first time I saw the cat lying in a corner of the room, looking dead. A small rug of an animal.

—Is Trader all right? I asked.

—I gave him too much of the tranquilizer. By mistake, Jane said. Then she picked up the box of pens and spilled them onto the table as if she were about to read a fortune with yarrow sticks. I wanted to say I miss Franny, that it seems impossible that the house will be sold, that it isn't necessary to dump all the pens out.

I thought it was the large business of settling Franny's estate that had them so keyed up. I'd seen this before: the sense of separation people can feel from themselves or each other when sorting the objects of the past. My boss often said you have to have a particular deficit of emotion to move freely through other people's lives. Some families pay the auction house to go over every last thing of their relative's. Letters, photos, spice jars, closets full of clothes, carried off in plastic bags for salvage or trash until they get down to the things they can sell. It's a stupid way to break down, but I never wanted another career. Even if I'm left to wonder if strangers will rake through my things eventually.

Just then Mona ran down the stairs carrying one of Franny's ivory jars from the matched set on her dressing table. She sprinkled face powder everywhere. Livvy ran after her until she saw me, then slowed to a walk and went over to look in a suitcase for something. This was the first summer she had made dramatic alterations to her appearance. The ear cuffs, the hair, the piercings, the black clothes.

Jane took the powder away.

—Hi girls, I said.

—Hi Mat, Mona said.

—Mattie, Livvy corrected her. Hey.

—Hey, I said.

She surfaced with a pink swimsuit, which she handed to Mona, who held it up so I could read the words emblazoned on the front: LOVES TO SWIM.

Mike winked at Livvy. Then he turned to me and said:

—We should invite the neighbors over for dinner tomorrow night.

He seemed eager to include me in things.

—To get in the mood? Jane said.

But I wasn't sure which mood she referred to, and I knew she didn't want me quizzing her, and it didn't matter to me if we had a dinner party or not. Mike didn't say anything, went out to the deck.

While Jane unpacked, I looked around the living room. The early-afternoon train came through heading north. It rode Franny's house like an act of nature. A familiar door above the stove always swung partway open with the vibrations. Franny used to cut sticky-back tape into dots and squares to fasten down her sculptural pieces. The yellow, cracked adhesive patches were still in place, stuck to the bookshelves. They no longer held the objects they were intended to safeguard

As Jane searched for swim fins and Livvy and Mona robbed the linen closet of towels, I watched Mike. I thought he had given up smoking, but there was a cigarette in his mouth. He bent each match outside the matchbook cover, lit it, and waved the book until it went out. As he stood there, I was aware that the deck looked more like a container than an open platform.

The house was right on the beach and the visibility was good that day. The coast runs west to east midway between Point Conception and Port Hueneme. The ocean is due south and in the summer people prop their chairs, slather up, let their toddlers go nude, wrestle with kayaks. Kids line up their boards like Cadillac Ranch. Dogs run in packs.

It was low tide, so there were fifty feet of beach at most and coastal access for all. Of course sometimes the beach disappeared entirely and the water pounded the lower decks. A newspaper left out could turn to a bit of papier-mâché stuck to a railing. The houses ranged from the substantial to the badly weathered, mostly wood framed. There was the pseudo-Spanish one of stucco, and a couple of blue-and-white nautical designs with overloaded themes.

Franny had owned her place down to the retaining wall. In winter she heaped sandbags around the pilings to keep her house from being carried out to sea. The lower deck had been rebuilt three separate times after bad storms. Flooring and carpet ripped up and replaced. Yet each summer when we arrived, her house was back in order.

I was eight when I met Jane. She was nine. My parents and I stayed at a rental a few doors down. It was always different at our house. Impermanent. Fragile. The kind of place where you could stiff a landlord on the last month's rent.

It was important to keep everything picked up, especially between my bedroom door and the bunks, so Lois, my mother, wouldn't trip in the dark. When she came home, she sometimes woke me to say good-night, sending out an exhaust of salt, peppermint candies, and gin as she spoke. She asked if I had spent time on my workbooks, if I had kept myself out of trouble. I said yes and yes, and when I attempted to sit up in the dark, she put a cool hand on my forehead, as if I might have a temperature.

I could make out the outline of her hair, brittle from the ocean, and I knew her lips were stung by weather. In daylight they were almost white, sometimes blistered. If she had something to say about children who hide in abandoned refrigerators or men who fall into elevator shafts, this was where she whispered to me, often drifting off and not quite finishing her stories. My mother gave me this advice: *If you have to jump from a burning building, leap second. Let someone else go first. This gives the men with the nets a chance to study the wind direction and velocity.*

Once she held up a piece of paper. There was a wheel in the center, my name in the upper left-hand corner, my birth date. Lois said: *I talked with a woman today. And she looked at your chart. She wants you to know that something will happen around travel . . . or a car. That was it. A car will change your life. It has to do with the planet Pluto. You're overloaded with Pluto.*

While she pointed to the black ink marks, I lay still, imagining a wheel rolling over me, flattening me to sleep. *You understand, don't you? This woman knows a good deal about these things. You should hear what she said about me.* Then Lois pulled herself up and receded into the hall, as if she hadn't been there.

For years I pictured a collision that would slow traffic around me. I saw where my lungs would puncture, heard the radio I couldn't turn off, stared at my foot impaled on the brake. I was aware that the orange reflective triangles would be placed around my car. I didn't understand at the time that predictions swerve and take on whole other meanings. There was a car, but no accident, no death. Unless you call love an accident. I don't.

three

The morning Jane left, I crawled into bed with Mike and didn't wake up until the midmorning express vibrated the French doors of the second-floor deck. Mike was propped up on one elbow, watching me. He looked amused, probably thought Jane and I were having him on. Maybe he was employing that simple carnival trick of his: to guess the weight of a head. Mike had worked on a midway one summer during college, and he had gotten pretty good at sizing up a person by the pound. But he wasn't reliable then and gave away too many stuffed cats and cloth dolls.

—Holding Jane's place? he laughed.

I sat up against the bolster, and launched into a nervous rap about the Jaguar. He leaned into me as I talked openly about the canvas top and the broken mechanism. We both liked machinery, how a good piece of equipment works, but I could only distract him so long, and I ran myself out detailing that car. Mike unraveled his pajamas from the covers, slipped into the bottoms, and got out of bed.

—Shout if I get warm.

He looked under the dust ruffle, stepped in and out of the bathroom, checked behind the yellow stuffed chair. When he came back to bed, he took my hand and said:

—I give.

—I tried to stop her.

He looked at my head again. I felt it lift off my neck and go onto the scale.

—She left the girls' insurance cards. Took two bags. I should have woken you. I haven't slept for . . . She's probably in San Luis Obispo by now. Paso Robles. This looks so bad. I couldn't think.

I watched the gill-like movement of his jaw, the small muscles tensing and relaxing. He balled up his pajama top and threw it across the room, and said:

—Fuck.

Then he laughed to himself.

—It's okay, Mike said. I lifted the receiver on the old white princess phone sitting on the bedside table, but it slipped from my hand and dropped to the rug.

—I'll try her cell, I said, unwinding the cord and starting over.

—She won't answer.

I hung the phone up.

—Did she go north?

—No. I mean, I don't know.

—Which car?

—The Jaguar.

—Is it too early for a drink?

He knew where Franny had kept her gin and brought it

back to bed. I took a sip, watched him, waiting for something other than the weary, almost luminous look he gets
after being up all night editing. For years Mike had made
documentaries. Exquisite, quirky things. My favorite was
the man fixing a VW Bug who talked about his six ex-
wives while he gapped the plugs and set the timing, his
lone voice working like a chorus in a Greek tragedy. He
said:

—You have to feel like you came out here for nothing.

—Don't worry about me. Maybe the police could . . .

He touched one of my eyebrows, as if it were out of
place.

It's okay? I thought. Sometimes Mike suffered from the
same kind of melancholy that overtakes me, so I understood that at least. And I understood his way of protecting
me. He lost his sister when he was fifteen. But, *it's okay?*
The blue bottles on Franny's dressing table sent out light.
The fog had burned off a good deal. It was the first clear
sky since our arrival, but that was how June was, unlimited
fog with a few breaks. I hoped it would be all right where
Jane drove.

—This is what she does. She drives off, he said.

I realized his eyes used to be a true, faded color. Now
they looked blue like laundry soap. I looked for contact
lenses as he gazed toward the islands, but I didn't see any. I
couldn't understand the way he'd aged. It wasn't that his
face was waxy or taut, injected or stitched into place; it was
unchanged. Changed, unchanged. I played with this like a
power surge—lights coming up, blacking out.

—Aren't you blind without your glasses?

—I can see you better this way, he said.

He moved his thumb over my right palm, not far from the spot where this random line bisects the lifeline and another line, the three lines forming a triangle if I flatten my hand out as a palm reader would. But instead he formed my hand into a small basin, as if he were going to pour something there. Once again he assured me that Jane was fine, that I shouldn't worry.

—We have to keep it low-key for the girls, he said, but his words and his mouth worked at different speeds now.

—Her disappearance, he said, as if I hadn't understood.

I probably had that stretched-awkward smile I get. We both took another drink.

—We could say she's gone to look for architectural salvage, I said.

—We're knee-deep in architectural salvage.

—But she has her time away, right? Conferences?

I began to feel my own break between phrasing and delivery. As I watched his face, I picked up something of Jane in the ticking of the feather pillows, mixed with her grandmother's oily scent. I looked at his chest. I felt like the girl in Duras's *The Lover,* when she was about to touch the man's chest for the first time. I offered to stay a couple of extra days, make some headway on Franny's stuff. Then I caught myself and quickly wound back to the girls.

We agreed that it would be plausible for Jane to go off and work for a while in seclusion. She had a commission designing sets for a version of *Peter Pan,* in Boston. Mike would hide her drawings.

He picked up the knotted ends of my nightgown ties and rolled them between his fingers, letting them drop against my chest.

—Can you really make any knot? he asked.

—I know knots, I said.

My father had taught me dozens of sailor's knots.

—And flags, I said. Capitals. By-products. My mother and her fucking workbooks.

—I thought you did scrapbooks.

—Those too.

I rushed to tell him everything I could about the articles I clipped. On a variety of subjects.

—I know. I could tell you where tulips spring up on Dutch maps.

I put my hand on his cheek and he said:

—I'd rather see a knot.

I tried to do something with the nightgown ties, but they were a little short.

He kissed my neck, just below my left ear, as I fiddled.

If Livvy were awake she was in the clock room, across the hall, listening to the passage of time, stubbornly holding on to her bladder. She was like Jane, hated to get out of bed in the morning. I wondered if she drifted when things got crazy. If her subtle body fled when it was under too much pressure, the way mine does. I knew she had her antenna and it's possible she could pick up sounds through the heating grate. Not that you could receive whole words that way, certainly not with the noise of the clocks, but Mike and I whispered nonetheless.

—I should go downstairs, I said.

—I know, he said, but touched my leg.

—There are people who eat tulips to calm down, I said.

—Tulip eaters, he said and slid his hand between my thighs.

I thought about bringing up the friend who slept with her second husband the night of her first husband's funeral, but I guessed that was a random thing, and let it go.

—We're both a little bereft right now, I said.

—This isn't about that.

—No?

—No.

Mike slowly pulled my nightgown up.

—I know how to draw kitchen triangles, I offered.

—That's why I've always loved you, Mattie.

—I have stats on gun-related deaths. Skee-ball accidents. Nothing on car flights. Less on why we drive toward collision.

I wanted to take my rental car and find Jane out in the state of California and bring her home, keep myself from going anywhere else. I wanted to climb onto his lap and stay on at freeway speeds.

He wetted my right nipple with his tongue. I looked at the small indentations on either side of his nose, from his glasses, as I tried to breathe. I pressed a baby finger into one of them. It fit perfectly, like a tiny shoe.

—Tell me one of your stories, he said.

That was what we did. We told each other stories.

—Okay. There was a woman who fucked the *David* once. That guy I knew in college, you remember Stuart, he told me that.

The light pressure of Mike's teeth, the way his tongue flicked. I thought of a ruby-throated hummingbird. But I proceeded with my story.

—I'm . . . not sure if he meant the false David near the Uffizi or the real David in Galleria dell'Accademia. But I hadn't been to Italy . . . then, and I think I was a little naïve about security. But I like picturing that . . . otherworldly event: the woman seeming to . . . float upward, maybe she used . . . a rope ladder, or had a harness or swing, maybe she had help . . . from friends. In either case, she must have ascended when the guards were changing shifts. I feel certain she held on to him . . . like a moth to a wool blanket . . . until the first shout and the hands . . . that plucked her off.

Mike slid his hand into the bottoms of my shortie pajamas. I closed my eyes and began to float. Just before my head hit the ceiling, I heard the door handle twist back and forth.

—There's something I have to watch! Mona shouted from the other side of the door.

Mike lifted his head.

—I'll be there in a few minutes, honey. Turn on the TV in the living room.

We listened to the weight of Mona's descent.

—Fate? Mike asked, as if he were offering me a soft drink.

The TV went on downstairs: *loud.*

Though I didn't ask, he told me not to worry about Livvy. She wouldn't be up for a while. She had stayed up very late.

He said he wanted to see every knot I knew how to make later. I wasn't sure when later was, but I knew he wasn't either. So I agreed to later.

Then Mike got up, kissed me once more, and soon the shower went on.

I found one of Jane's robes. A pocket held a scrap of paper with this message: *Nan wants the tea service.* I wasn't sure who had written it. In college, after Jane had dropped architecture and started sleeping with Mike, she'd changed her handwriting. I thought she wanted to move away from rendering. But now I understand she was trying to copy Mike.

As I slipped out the door and inched down the stairs to the first floor, I realized that he was soaping himself, bending under the low showerhead. Large enough for three, the stall had been plumbed to hit body parts below five feet. It only bothered me when I had to shampoo. But Mike was over six-foot-one, Jane five-eight.

The blue satin cuffs of her bathrobe slid past my fingertips, the bottom hem made a petal on the floor, almost bridal. She was probably passing through central California as Mike's hot water ran and I knotted the robe ties. Inhaling fertilizer, the scent of developing artichokes, she would pull off at the exit and head toward a stand. Probably the one with a mural of dancing artichokes on the side. The kind of place that also sells honey, walnuts, medjool dates. She would sit in the car for a while and try to decide if she should leave the 101 and take back roads instead. There wasn't any hurry if she had no idea where she was going. Of course she could have just turned around, pulled the Jaguar into the garage, found me down in the living room with Mona, and never questioned my wearing her robe.

There was a guy who killed himself on the 101 by taking a shotgun and wiring it to the shaft of the steering wheel. When he was ready, and I have no idea what that means, he pulled on the metal loop he had attached to the trigger. His car fishtailed and launched into the oncoming lanes. He took out a teenaged girl who had planned an acting career in what-the-hell Hollywood. Her boyfriend had just detailed her Toyota Celica. She was wearing jeans and a pink sweater, no shoes. Her ankle bracelet had the boyfriend's name engraved on it. It was hard not to think about that kind of stuff after Jane left.

four

Sometimes Mona just started spinning. For no particular reason. While Mike took his shower, I watched her spin in Franny's living room. Her hair flew out, her feet made a dish in the carpet, her skirt ringed the planet of her body.

Livvy came downstairs in her blue silk kimono. She looked like she should be filmed that way, with her blue hair. The Gaugin light on her face. I don't think she wanted to be a presence like her mother. But she was. She straddled the Aldo chaise lounge, her legs draped over the wooden frame. The cat, Trader, curled at the end.

Mona flew onto the couch, pulled herself up, and started spinning again.

On the fifth effort at revolution, Livvy patiently said:

—I think we're all getting a little dizzy.

This time Mona dropped to the ground, her eyes fat and shiny as hard-boiled eggs.

—Did you see how fast I went, Mattie?

Livvy tried not to smile. Mona wobbled to her feet and began to spin again. Whether I stared right into the center of events or looked out to the frayed edge, she was time out of control. Certainly out of mine, perhaps out of Jane's. I don't know if I can speak for the rest.

Livvy hit the remote and the barking laughter went off and the screen went gray. Just then, Mona lost her balance and went flying, landing hard against Livvy's right leg, pressing it against the chaise lounge. The cat launched off the end.

—Mona! Livvy complained.

—Can I get a bandage? I asked.

—No, I'm all right.

I crouched beside Livvy and asked if she wanted ice. Livvy had Jane's complexion. Sometimes I stared at it too long. She had Jane's energy, and Mike's eyes, constantly framing. But she had her own blue hair, select piercings.

Before she could say anything, Mona told me:

—You have to crush the ice cubes.

I couldn't find the hammer in the pantry. I tried pounding the ice with a jar of dry-roasted peanuts, but knew it might shatter. I got a box of Popsicles out of the freezer. Back in the living room, I looked at the bruise coming up and wrapped a dish towel around the box.

—It's really okay, Livvy said.

—Can I have a Popsicle? Mona asked.

I had to list the flavors for Mona more than once to be understood in TV-time, since the set was on again. She picked raspberry.

—Can you peel off the wrapper?

Livvy said she'd do that and I went off to the kitchen to make the girls' breakfast. I knew they liked the croissants that pop out of a tube and bake in an oven. Livvy and I appreciated the golden look, Mona wanted hers pale and doughy. Jane had picked up several tubes, which she had stored in the vegetable chiller. I made eggs, whipped up orange juice in the blender to give it the froth Mona wanted, and called the girls.

At the table Livvy pushed her eggs around with her knife. Periodically, Mona gave her sister's plate a little bump.

Livvy didn't react. Mona did it again.

As I lifted the glasses to wipe up the orange-juice rings on the table, I told them their mother had gone on a short working trip to keep up with her *Peter Pan* deadline. Mona stopped what she was doing and watched Livvy's unbroken stare as she tracked my cleanup job. Livvy asked for details. I made up a couple of things to satisfy her. I couldn't tell if she knew something, or suspected something.

Mona revved into a conversation about *Peter Pan,* saying she loved Tiger Lily, stressing the importance of the clock inside the alligator's belly, the way it hypnotized Captain Hook. She loved the cartoon.

—Dad knows how to hypnotize people, she said. I asked him to hypnotize me, but he said it's too powerful.

—I understand, I said, wiping down the stove.

—He can even hypnotize someone while they're driving.

Mona poked her index finger into her croissant while I was left to picture this.

Livvy went out to the deck. She had barely touched her plate.

. . . . . .

Mike overshot breakfast by a half hour. I had already opened my laptop and logged on to the Internet. An e-mail from my former employer, closer to making that job offer. Trying to move some money around to pay me.

Pop-ups. Urgings to gamble, to save, to insure myself, to lose weight, to find a car. One e-mail from a prospective human being, a leftover from a time when I had rashly listed myself with a dating service. He was a tall, bearded man who had answered most of his survey questions with: *I'll tell you later.*

Do you have children? *I'll tell you later.*

He wanted to know in this, our first and only exchange, if I'd consider relocation overseas. He had so much love to give, he said.

When Mike came downstairs I blanked the screen. Sometimes he exuded a manic, survivalist energy, as though he needed to get back to a delivery truck and all he wanted was a signature in the right place. That was how he hit the carpet in the living room. Maybe he was looking for something but didn't know what to lift, how to pry it up. He gathered the mail and put it down unopened.

Mona tossed a red throw pillow at Livvy's head.

—Mona. Settle down, Mike said.

—She's driving me a little crazy, Livvy said to her father.

—We'll go for a swim in a while.

—Mona, you *need* to go for a swim, Livvy said.

Mona went off to look for her swim noodles. Mike stood by the French doors. I couldn't see his expression with the backlight. I didn't understand his wavering movements, as if he were standing before a carnival mirror. He came back to where I was seated at the table, supported his weight on his arms, his back to the girls. He looked as if he wanted to say something.

Just then Mona returned to the living room, noodleless, and threw another pillow at Livvy's stomach. I went off to the kitchen so Mike could work it out. There I curled my toes around the handle of a bottom drawer. The girls' documents were still where I had buried them, under the cloth napkins; I hadn't gone entirely mad. When I came back to the living room, I handed him a cup of coffee and some sugar packets.

Then I lifted one of Mona's legs to get to the marble box on the coffee table. Some filtered cigarettes, some menthol, probably all stale. I think he took one to please me.

—I'll be right back, I said.

I threw together the kinds of food stocked for such occasions: a couple of easy spreads for the leftover croissants, smoked salmon, strawberries with stems in place. The cheese I put on the breadboard with a single slice cut off. I tied on one of Franny's party aprons before I realized what I was doing and returned it to its hook. I primped in the downstairs bathroom, where I found the old cosmetics. The pressed powder smelled of overuse, a skin slicked on its surface. The lipstick was a hideous gumdrop-red. I gave up and returned to the living room, still in Jane's robe. I thought about true and false radiance.

The girls had gone to suit up. I watched Mike blow on his coffee, and look at me. We both noted the boxes. I tried to think about the chaos of sorting, but my mind began to stutter and misfire as we stood there. I fantasized him sending the girls out to the beach in a little while, that he would draw the blinds, climb out of his clothes, look half-heartedly for his swim trunks. I thought of objects from Pompeii. The bowl of a pipe carved into the shape of a man. I wanted to take a long draw from the pipe.

I started to hand him something to eat, but one of the strawberries rolled to the edge of the plate. I tipped it back toward the center as if I were trying to get a tiny silver ball into the dip of a child's game. Watching it come to rest, I realized I had become awkward with him.

—What are you doing? he laughed.

—Balancing.

I said something about the beach being empty. Not a dog out.

Nearly everyone along the row of beach houses had a dog; at least it seemed that way when they were driving the non-dog owners insane. Every now and then the strays. The fog had moved out to the islands. I became aware of pelicans diving into the ocean. A whole division of them climbing and bombing in straight vertical lines.

—Look.

But he *was* looking.

—I'm not much of a help, he said. I'll get with it.

I forgot that I still had the food extended toward him until I felt the plate drop from my hands.

Trader lifted his head from the spot where he had curled, expressed little interest. Mike helped me pick up the food. He briefly took one of my hands. I felt the pressure of his ring against my bones.

He leaned into me, put his mouth next to my ear, and said:

—You're doing that thing.

—What thing? I asked.

—Search and rescue.

—Maybe.

He whispered:

—*She wouldn't rescue you.*

We broke apart before Livvy started down the stairs. She seated herself in front of my laptop and refreshed the screen. I realized that she was looking at the men I had once spent hours poring over, reading through heights and weights and drinking habits. She smiled to herself and pulled the lid down so the screen went cold and then she went into the kitchen. Mona appeared and slumped on the couch. Mike gave her a kiss and stepped onto the deck. I joined Mona.

—I wonder what it feels like to not be alive, she said.

—There are theories on that, Mona.

—I mean, before you're in your mom's belly, just before you get inside.

—Ah.

—I wonder what that's like, she said.

—Yeah, me too.

Mike stood with his feet far apart, which gave him the appearance of stability, a lowered center of gravity. He had had an affair years ago, which Jane said he mostly regretted. She said he'd changed after that. Focused more intensely on his work. Restrained, she called him. I sometimes think she missed his wilder self. But it was hard to sort out. He had never changed the way he was with me.

His pants and jacket flapped against his body as he looked toward the harbor. It was Wet Wednesday: the sailboats would be racing. I don't believe he was talking to me but I thought I heard him say something.

But then I've caught his voice before, when he wasn't around. It's come through Jane in their dark living room back in Boston. If she called, it was after her family had gone to sleep. She'd have a sudden urge to read a paragraph from one of his old letters to me. Or she'd talk about the film he was working on or what they'd said over dinner. It felt as if she were trying to convince herself of something. I pictured her sitting on the couch in her robe, gazing at her own reflection in the glass doors that lead out to their backyard. Staring long enough for a natural split to occur. I imagine she saw the part of herself capable of rolling the sliders back and taking off out the side gate, leaving her sandals where she'd stepped out of them. Then she'd let her eyes go weary and see the woman who was fixed there, pairing and folding the girls' socks as we talked.

Maybe she really did want my seminomadic life.

Once, driving through central Illinois, on the lookout for a motel with air conditioning, I found a small circus in an open field. The tent had so many holes the lights beamed from it like bright worms in the dark. Parking my car, I stepped into the flight of frantic insects. The show was half over. Many of the benches were empty, the toys unsold.

The tent fluttered, and the smell of overcooked hot dogs rose into the air. It was the knife-thrower and his slender redheaded assistant who intrigued me. She was fastened to a huge crimson wheel at the ankles, wrists, and waist. The man gave the wheel a mighty crank. The woman spun faster and faster until she became nothing more than a bull's-eye. The audience gasped each time he threw a knife at the wheel. When it came to rest, she was silhouetted with knives—one blade even pinned the edge of her dress. He released her and they kissed.

five

When Jane blew away, my mind fired in all directions, hitting every available memory, hoping to dislodge a solid reason for her flight. What's that Jarrell poem about the ball turret gunner?

Conversations, small, abrupt gestures, missed cues, blind alleys. I sought all of them.

After a while I felt like I was watching towers of stacked DVDs to find an actor in her early, obscure parts, to see if she had stared straight into the camera at first or looked away, if her facial gestures corresponded with her lines, if she looked real then or if she became more real.

I went into all the rooms of Jane's psychic house, over her entire property. Though I thought I knew where the worms were buried in her backyard, I ripped up her lawn and laid the pink bodies of childhood end to end. I recalled conversations we had in high school when we analyzed each other's dreams using a book. We did that kind of thing, even though the answers were skewed toward sex and death, and we were gullible. When we were in our

early twenties, I sat next to Jane as she had her chart cast
in a mall in Los Angeles. Later she said the astrologer
had gotten her eighth house mixed up. I wasn't sure
what that meant but I understood her concerns. There
was something in the eighth house having to do with
the absent father. I stayed up late to read comic books
or true mysteries to her when she was in a bad way
about him.

I had always worried about the way Jane would take
Franny's death. Maybe that was about my own sense of
loss, and maybe I should have understood that a lot sooner.
But when she called to tell me the news, she reported it
factually, which angered me. Though I don't think I con-
veyed this over the phone.

Franny had stepped in front of an oncoming train to
rescue her dog, Meiko, a sweet but undereducated Irish
Setter. Meiko had a beautiful coat, which Franny attrib-
uted to the avocados she fed her daily, and she was known
for rubbing against the kitchen door if she sensed she was
going to be released into the world. So Franny often
walked her away from the beach to avoid other dogs. If she
leashed her, Meiko tugged as if Franny were on wheels, so
she had learned to leave the leash off.

I often thought of Katharine Hepburn when I saw
Franny launch off in her athletic shoes and baggy pants,
Meiko bounding ahead. They liked to walk behind the
houses, down the alley, and cross through a break in the

hedge. From there the path opens into a neighborhood with some bungalow-style houses and plenty of hydrangeas.

The discussion at the funeral was that she had acted on heroic impulse. Mike had talked with someone from the Southern Pacific Railroad. The conductor kept a log with a list of injuries and deaths along his route. He had the date, time, and a note about reaching for the brake. Meiko was placed in the hard clay of a friend's property on Mountain Drive after hours of digging. Franny had purchased a plot in the Santa Barbara Cemetery years ago. I flew in, tried to make myself useful.

The cemetery is set on a mesa some thirty feet above a nude beach. That afternoon, we stood in the middle of the road that meandered through the grounds. I looked at Jane's straight posture, one shoe pushed against the curb, her calf muscle flexed. She looked like someone preparing for a run.

The offshore winds had picked up. Loose strands of her hair moved across her face. As she pulled them away, I noticed Franny's emerald. The band was too big for Jane's finger. I worried it might fly off and roll against a flat headstone, and into the lawn. I was aware of the eucalyptus, the smell.

Jane had just taken on the *Peter Pan* commission. She said:

—Peter Davies threw himself in front of a train.

—The guy Barrie based his play on?

—I think the character overtook him. Imagine being a grown man, people taunting you with: *Where's your shadow, Peter?*

I was afraid any argument would cement the concept of Franny's fragility in Jane's mind, so I let it go.

The girls were a few feet away in the black limo. Mona sent the windows up and down, Livvy stared off. Everyone else had gone. Mike had taken a couple of Franny's friends home, the ones who didn't drive anymore. I thought Jane was about to say something regarding her daughters, but she stopped when the chauffeur emerged from the limo.

With the look of someone who's forgotten to make a phone call, Jane took a sudden interest in his movements. He was bowlegged, and she kept her eyes on him as he walked over and stopped in front of a mausoleum.

He removed his cap and tucked it under one arm. He had good arms. I imagine he worked out regularly. He fiddled with his cigarettes until he had one lit. Behind him were the cemetery's World War II graves, the concrete wall with the chain-link fencing on top, and the large sky.

—You getting a headache from that eucalyptus? I asked.

—How long do you think we could make that man stand there? she asked, sizing him up.

—We have the limo for a couple of hours.

—But is that a couple of hours driving or standing around?

The wind had picked up since morning. The pine, the fan palms were all in motion. She took off her black sunglasses and looked at me. I tried, as always, not to stare at the scar that cut across one eyebrow. I was relieved to see her expression relax.

—Why don't the girls and I take a taxi back to the

house? You can take the limo through the foothills. It's a perfect day. Go up to Mountain Drive.

I ignored the perfect day.

—There must be somewhere you'd like to go, Jane said.

She put her glasses back on. A string of clouds floated across their surface. She wore a dress with spring flowers. It had a notable décolletage in the back. Something appropriate for a wedding, a luncheon. I said:

—Why don't we go back to the house? I'll put some lunch together.

She nodded toward the driver.

—Maybe I should take the drive. Might be a kick. You know what they say about bowlegged men, she said.

I looked out to the islands, caught in a distorted lens. This was Jane but exaggerated.

—You don't get how funny this is, do you? she said.

—No, I'm probably missing something.

I moved to one of the open windows of the limo. Livvy was sitting with Mona on the floor now, showing her how to fold Franny's blue memorial leaflets into airplanes. They didn't bother to look up. I returned to Jane. She was facing the ocean now, and I think she was making some kind of calculation.

—They're doing fine, I said.

—Pretty choppy. But I'm sure the girls will want to go for a swim. I could take them out to the float.

For years the Miramar Hotel had anchored a large wooden float a hundred yards out in the water for its guests.

—If the lifeguard doesn't chase you away, I said.

—Fuck the lifeguard. Fuck your safe life.

It wasn't until later, after I'd worn that phrase down, tumbling it in my mind, that I heard its prayer-like quality. But I was weary, running without sleep as well.

—I can't know what you're going through. . . .

—That's right.

—But you think my world feels safe with her gone.

I had talked with Franny every couple of weeks on the phone, all of my adult life and most of my adolescent years. Maybe I had never told Jane about this, didn't think I needed to. Maybe Franny didn't freight this information.

Jane left me and walked toward Franny's grave. Her new high heels made her movements difficult, and after a few yards she took them off and left them on the grass. She dropped beside the grave, moving so quickly I thought she might fall in. I could imagine her doing that—falling in, laughing like a crow, warning everyone off. But she just sat there beside her grandmother.

One of the aunts, staring at that long, half-naked back, had said something unkind to me about Jane's outfit at the funeral. Jane liked to keep herself in good shape and I think this added gall to the aunt's complaint.

The longer I looked at Jane, the more she seemed like a woman having a picnic on a lawn. She leaned on one arm, legs pulled close to her body. The eucalyptus began to cloy, the sun was overbright. I had left my sunglasses in the back of the limo and could only squint now, a migraine had started. Jane appeared and disappeared as pressures built in my cranium.

That was when I saw her drive off in the Jaguar. Only in this version, Franny was in the passenger seat, Jane's father in the back with both of his arms along the top edge of the leather upholstery, straining to hear their conversation.

I made an effort to get oxygen the way my therapist encouraged when the small visions approached. I opened a passenger door to the limo. Mona smiled at me.

—You okay in there? I asked.

Livvy sailed past me to get out of the car. Her hands were filled with small paper aircraft. Mona followed, trying to keep up in her white shoes.

They attempted to fly their planes from the cliff, the craft forced back by the wind toward the gravestones. I looked back at Jane. The thought occurred to me that this was her way of making all of us wait: the girls, the driver, me. When I swung round again, Mona was inches from the edge. A clod of dirt broke free near one of her shoes. It fell toward the beach. I stepped over a couple of headstones so I could come up behind her, slowly.

—Scoot back this way, Mona, honey. You're too close to the edge.

I was a foot away now and stifled the impulse to grab her. Livvy seemed untroubled by the height but took Mona's hand and moved her back a little.

Mona suddenly grew aware of her surroundings. I took her other hand.

—I'll have to teach you the names of the shorebirds, I said.

—You know some of them, don't you, Mona? Livvy said.

—Pelicans, terns.

—And the water currents? You know about them? I asked.

—Do you have any more paper? Livvy asked.

I rummaged in my purse.

—Kleenex.

—You can't make airplanes out of Kleenex, Mona said.

Livvy pulled her springy hair into a ponytail, looked over at her mother for a while.

—I'm going to sit up front, Livvy said and went back to the limo.

—I get to wear Franny's high heels, Mona said.

We got in the back of the car. It was difficult to see Livvy behind the dark shield that separated us. She hadn't shown any real signs of mourning. I had no idea if this was to be expected at fourteen. Maybe she would experience ongoing mourning the way Jane had for her father.

Mona stretched her legs out on the seat, her shoe bottoms pressed against my beige skirt. The driver ground a cigarette into the base of the mausoleum.

When Jane joined us, she positioned herself so Mona could put her head in her lap. Mona gazed out the sunroof as if her job was to go blind with patience.

The driver returned to the limo. Soon we headed back through the cemetery's roads.

—Knock on the glass, Mattie, Jane said, motioning toward the chauffeur's window. When it was lowered, she said:

—Are you all right, sweetheart?

Livvy made no reply. But the chauffeur smiled at her. Maybe his look was a little suggestive.

—I wish you'd slip back here and snuggle, Jane said, patting the seat next to her.

—I'm watching the odometer, Livvy said.

—We can go swimming all afternoon if you like.

—I'd like to go swimming, Mona said, yawning.

—My suit disintegrated, Livvy said, and gave the chauffeur a look.

—Livvy's on the swim team. The chlorine . . . I'm sure we could talk this pumpkin into going shopping, Jane said. Her voice a silk that began to unravel.

Livvy reached over and pushed the button, closing the chauffeur's window. Jane ran her fingers through Mona's hair and mumbled something about the gravestone.

—I don't think there are any rules about how quickly it's done, I said.

—But what do you say?

—Keep it simple. Name, dates.

I fiddled with the silver ashtray on my armrest.

—Name, dates, Mona repeated absently before shutting her eyes and drifting toward sleep.

—Livvy blames me for everything.

—I don't think . . .

Her look stopped me. She turned to watch for her grandmother's grave. Soon enough she rested her head on my shoulder.

. . . . . .

My mother, Lois, once pulled her head out of a *Life* magazine, in the middle of a flat afternoon, and posed one of her riddles to my father and me: *If death brings investigation, what does life bring?*

My mother was staring at a photo of John and Yoko on the magazine cover. I think my father was about to venture an answer but changed his mind.

More investigation? I asked, hoping to please someone.

But the topic was dropped, and the dull air continued to circulate through the ducts of our rental.

After I became an appraiser, Lois claimed I had gotten my investigative powers from her. She was a decent generalist, always on to some bit of knowledge in a condensed or abridged book. My father wanted her to go on a game show, make some real money.

But I know it was Franny who pollinated that part of my brain.

six

I've read accounts of mothers who forget their children in stores, walk out to their cars with groceries, linens, waffle irons—leave their kids in the cart. An hour or more goes by until it hits them.

Maybe Jane had a different brand of crazy going. The kind where you reach into the pockets of the car doors and find all the maps gone.

She called my cell the day after she took off. It was late in the day and I was getting takeout from the Mexican restaurant near Von's. The plain rice with the pollo asada and melted cheese on top for Mona, salsa "from the back" for Livvy, the chimichanga for Mike. I watched the owner's son stuff white paper bags with chips.

At first I thought Jane was in a restaurant as well. She liked those places where they serve fifteen flavors of low-content pie. It's a weakness of hers, like her need for milk. I was certain she'd be looking out at the Jaguar in the parking lot, trying to keep an eye on the luggage. She would forget the phone number several times before she was able to dial, she never wrote numbers down. I imagined her sitting at the counter, ordering another slice of the Boston cream so she could pencil out combinations of numbers on her paper napkin.

But when I put the receiver to my ear, I didn't hear the sound of a knife scraping a pie tin. Instead the occasional car, the sound of her pauses. I reassured her and asked where she was and felt one of her Doppler effects drive through me. As the cars approached, I heard the higher tone. As they left her, a lower tone. Maybe she had stopped at a motel with a kidney-shaped pool and plastic buckets of ice, just to prop the door to her room open and think. She didn't like air conditioning. She asked about the girls again.

—They're fine. They're okay. Are you all right?

The cook ladled suisa onto the enchiladas.

—I had to ditch the Jaguar.

—You . . .?

I slid out of my sandals and brushed off the sand, rubbing one foot against the other.

—If you get a call from the Highway Patrol . . . I couldn't get the top up. It's on the shoulder, on Highway 101, just north of Salinas. This woman helped me with the bags, drove me until we found a car-rental place, she was very nice. You'll probably get a notice. Or you could have it towed if you want. I guess that would be the natural order of things.

—There's a highly underused term: *the natural order.*

—I'm going to this place called The Mystery Home tomorrow.

I gripped the phone in one hand and received the handles of two plastic bags full of takeout in the other while she told me that objects roll uphill in *The Mystery Home*.

—I've missed it entirely, I said.

The girl at the counter looked at me. I had raised my voice. She spooned the salsa into Styrofoam containers.

—You said the girls are fine?

—Mona misses you. And if I don't get back to Chicago, I'm going to miss this job. And if I miss this job, I'm going to crap out on my mortgage. And I wouldn't mind seeing my friends. There's a wedding next weekend and . . .

Her breathing had begun to change.

—Look, you have to talk to Mike, I said.

I could hear a fountain now, maybe water running into a pool. I wanted to hold her in place, fix her somewhere. The sound moved in and away from my ear.

—He's a dubious gift, isn't he?

—Mike is . . .

I heard a man call out on Jane's end, to see if someone needed a towel. I pictured him on the second floor of the motel, washed in yellow bug lights, his chest bare, swim trunks and inner tube in hand.

—Look, while I help keep the girls on track, and go through the estate, and have the Jag towed, and puzzle out why you keep giving Mike away, what will you be doing?

—There's a very large Paul Bunyan monument I want to see.

When I hung up on her, a vacuum crowded around the phone and the girl at the counter handed me the last of the takeout.

. . . . . .

As I drove back to the house, I realized my mother had liked everything about motels. And that she was almost available to me when we were on the road. She nestled the wrapped soaps around the socks in my suitcase so my things would smell nice. She ran her hands along the fold of the bed linen when she tucked me in. She asked me to come watch as she broke the paper band on the toilet bowl, which reminded her, she said, of her father's cigar bands when she was little. She wanted to get me to laugh, I think. We ate sandwiches on the courtyard picnic tables that she cleaned off with wet paper towels, and we bought loads of breakable souvenirs.

Lois sat at the pool's edge and stuck her legs in the water, threw hard rubber fish for me to dive down and retrieve. Sometimes I thought of my parents as people contained within a screen, visitors traveling back and forth in my view, stopping to fight, move a few boxes around, order cases from the liquor store, and then go off like TV sets shutting down. But when they were away from the impulse of sailboats and their upkeep, the yacht club and the shortwave, Lois would go out to the drugstore, read the sides of all the boxes, and bring back a semiperm kit designed to restore lost enthusiasm to my head. I was six when she spent hours winding my stringy hair around the rollers and squirting the noxious blue goo over them. As soon as I sprang with life, she would take me out to clothes shops, buy me a couple of new outfits, and see that the short-order cook wedged a cookie onto the plate of my hot-fudge sundae dish at the restaurant.

—Did you hear the waitress say how cute you look? Lois would say, lighting a cigarette and pushing out a halo of smoke that ringed me for a moment and broke up.

—Maybe this is the summer I'll teach you to sail, she said.

—Really?

I had my scrapbook out and a bottle of Elmer's, and I was pasting in a newspaper article about a firefighter who jumped one hundred feet off a building and didn't have a bruise. I had already filled one album and was on my second. I collected things about helicopter pilots who flew for the Red Cross, and men who dropped into tunnels and shafts to find small, wedged children underground. Lois had encouraged me. She knew Albert, my father, would be pleased.

—If the weather's right. And we aren't getting ready to race.

—I don't mind just being on board and watching. Just sitting there. I know how to duck.

—We'll see. Children fall off boats. We don't want that to happen because we're in the thick of things.

I drew the cookie out and attempted a smile.

—You're just like me when I was little, she said, and got up to look through the magazine rack.

I hoped I projected a subliminal all-right-ness when I arrived at Franny's with the takeout. All right that Jane was on her way to *The Mystery Home*. And all right that I thought obsessively of the dimple at the base of Mike's spine. I was relieved that conversation didn't really catch at the dining table and that I could simply spoon the salsa down my throat on crisp warm chips.

Soon enough Mike and I threw the containers away and straightened up the living room, trying not to collide. I wished for an elegant moment of physics that would take us into a separate, altered time. Until then we cleared dishes.

Mona went off to bed and Livvy went upstairs to bleach her hair in order to get the new primary color to adhere. I went out and sat on the stairs leading down to the beach, sometimes paying attention to the surf. Mike brought out a blender of margaritas and two salt-rimmed glasses. Mona's science kit was open in my lap, and I was trying to figure out how the parts fit in the case. Mike poured our drinks and reached behind me to set the blender down.

—Livvy said you've been Internet dating?

—Thank you, Livvy. Just contacting. No real dates. But I did receive an e-mail from a man in Waukegan who told me I'm *not* a babe and how happy this made him. He was enthralled, really. Wanted to get together. Maybe men in Waukegan are troubled by babes. You think there's a glut?

—Why are you wasting your time? I bet men hit on you all the time at work.

I had begun to shiver but remained fixed on the steps. I understood the tweezers and the slides, I just wasn't sure about the sandpaper. Mike gave me his leather jacket. It had his heat and the stitching Jane had done to repair the cuffs.

—The men who come to the auction house are looking for rugs, tables, items of torture. I think the sandpaper's for cleaning off the anodes, don't you?

—So what about this guy *Clark?*

I crossed my legs, shifted slightly. He put his cold feet next to mine, and I almost lost a petri dish.

—Did I ever tell you you remind me of John Cusack?

—Not a bad diversion.

—Okay. Clark's . . . Clark.

—Which means?

I could make the small batteries fit into the die-cut foam, but not the large ones. Two D batteries with clean anodes had no nest.

—Relatively insignificant.

Before he had a chance to break that down, I topped off our drinks and rerouted things.

—Did I ever tell you I get premonitions?

—Why wouldn't you tell me that?

—I don't think I've told anyone. They're not always reliable.

Mike showed me how to connect the two wires to the ends of the batteries and triangulate the wires to the bulb to make it light up. The red sky was clear to Santa Rosa Island.

He told me to close my eyes. I followed instructions and took a sip of my margarita.

—I want to do something with the salt on your lower lip, he said.

I found the salt with my tongue.

—Will you tell me later what you'd do?

—I'll demonstrate. Now, keep your eyes shut. I'm thinking of a color, he said.

—It doesn't work that way.

—Are you concentrating?

—I'm thinking of slipping my hands inside a cool zipper. But red. I see red.

I opened my eyes.

—I was thinking red.

—We are having a rather large sunset, Mike.

—Skip colors. Think of a number between . . . no, let's do cities. Major cities.

—I can't make it happen.

He rested a hand on my left knee.

—You have beautifully formed knees.

—Thank you.

—So tell me what it's like. To have a premonition.

—Sometimes it starts with a heightened sense of smell. Don't laugh. I can pick up bacon cooking three blocks away. Soil amendments a mile off.

—I thought those were your migraines.

—That's what I mean. They start with a migraine but then I'll get a vivid picture in my mind.

—Like a movie?

—More of a documentary.

—Those are never accurate.

—I don't hear voices. And I can't turn it on and off. If I could, I'd turn it off. It's just that sometimes, after a migraine comes on, I see something that's going to happen.

—This is wild.

—My father used to eat his dinner in front of the radio. Turning the dial on his shortwave the whole time, looking for signals from lost people. Sometimes it feels like I get one of those signals.

—Maydays from the Dead Sea?

There were two copper wires that had to be straightened out and a small bulb that looked like it might fit in a flashlight. I quickly unraveled the wires and forced everything back into the case any which way, the Styrofoam squeaking.

—The afternoon Franny died, before anyone told me, I was in a grocery store near my apartment. I knew the minute she had been hit by the train. I walked out and left a full cart sitting in the aisle. I went home and tried to reach her all afternoon. Then Jane called and told me what had happened.

—You knew she had been hit by a train?

—I had an image of her flying back from something, like a blast. She traveled for a long distance in the air, getting smaller and smaller, and I knew she was dead.

Mike put an arm around my shoulders.

—Do you . . .? Never mind, I said.

—No fair.

—Do you still sleep together?

—Not as much as you'd think.

—But you really talk, right?

—We have more shortcuts than actual talk.

I had assumed they still talked about everything, stayed up late to work in conversations, that they were successful archaeologists where love was concerned. Jane once showed me the lock on their bedroom door, put there so the girls wouldn't catch them in the act. I thought they had a sustained energy, effortless. But sometimes Mike had signaled me. I don't mean the kind of easy flirtation that happened. That was quick to toss off. I mean the thing you simply try to watch as it goes through, after you've boarded up your house.

When I found a way to tell him about the call, the Paul Bunyan remark, he laughed and said:

—Maybe she's looking for a bigger man.

—Very funny.

—Someone as big as her father.

—No one's that size.

—He adored Jane but he wasn't a very nice guy to her mother.

—I thought she was the source of their troubles, I said.

We debated the father's unhappiness for a while, as if we could come to a unified conclusion about a person neither of us had known but had both been influenced by. Finally I said I preferred the mythological father. The one Jane had placed in fluid time.

—Strong loyalties, he said.

—Waning.

We drank, he rubbed my arm. It was the kind of intimacy we had always had. But I was a little nervous that Livvy would come downstairs, dripping with blue dye, and see the subliminal.

—Would you say you have a whole life? I asked.

Mike laughed.

—I mean before this. Last week. Jane asked me that before she took off, if I had a whole life.

—What does that mean?

—I'm not sure.

—I think we need to take a walk, he said. I'll ask Livvy to watch Mona.

Mike ran upstairs and when he returned, we started down the beach. I wore one of those skirts Franny had saved for fiesta parties. The flashlight he had grabbed had a dim bulb that he hit against his leg repeatedly to fuel the beam. We walked down to the small scrubby field just before Fernald Point. It had once been a Chumash site. Jane had danced in its yellow grasses when we were girls. I had rimmed the edges, watching. Now it was socked in with fog.

I could barely make out the monument as Mike and I climbed the slope to level ground, the ocean eating away at the sand behind us. Mike went in and out of definition in the light. I felt the cool metal flask against my arm and I unscrewed the cap and swallowed. I heard him drink. The air had me shaking. Nervous. I put a palm on his chest, to steady myself. I drank until I warmed.

—I was thinking about that apartment you had on Beacon Hill, he said.

—That crazy roommate I had. Lucy, no, Lacy. The one

with bathroom concerns. I brushed my teeth too loudly or I wasn't supposed to spit when I was done. She liked sleeping in the tub with her boyfriend. We only had one bedroom.

—I almost crawled into that bedroom window once.

—When you and Jane were a couple?

—Yes.

—But I lived on the third floor.

—I parked my car in the alley. The blue Buick. I propped a ladder against the hood.

—Why didn't you ring the bell?

I felt the threads of embroidery against my thighs as Mike lifted my skirt. He kissed my face, talked in my right ear, in my head, right there.

—I wanted to surprise you.

—Why didn't you?

—I couldn't keep the ladder steady.

—Did you put a dent in your hood?

—A significant dent.

—If you had . . . crawled through my window . . . what would you have done?

—I would have performed . . . the hook and ladder on you, he said.

Then Mike moved down my torso as I stood in the dark air. My skirt dropped over his head. We made love like young dogs. Hooked. We stayed swollen and hooked as long as we could.

seven

Tripping backward. The day after I emerged at Franny's house with my rule-lined pads and pencils, Jane and I started in on the estate. My understanding was that she planned to be in the kitchen. And though I considered starting on the fine arts, I hit the safety of Franny's walk-in closet instead. I cleaned old tissues and mints and coins from purses. I set the lipsticks in a plastic bag for Mona, who had already gone around the house collecting them from the bathrooms. I put the best scarves and silk kimonos aside for Livvy. Franny wore the skinniest slacks, saved hats and belts for years.

I stepped out of the closet with a stack of blouses on hangers draped over my arms, surprised to find Jane propped up in Franny's bed. She had the old button tin in her lap and I watched her pry off the top. Maybe she planned to rescue individual buttons.

I dumped the blouses on the chair of the dressing table.

Jane moved over, making room for me in bed.

—Do you want to look through these before they go to the shelter? I asked.

She tipped her head slightly to make sure I understood that she had made a spot for me.

—Pass. Did I say I want you to have the Jaguar? I know how much you love it. I'll see if I can get anywhere with Nan. Mattie, you're making me nervous. Please sit down.

Jane wore a pair of shorts and a halter top that showed strap lines from her bathing suit. Some of her hair pinned up, some falling around her shoulders. Her face was waxy without makeup, almost vulnerable. I sat on the extreme edge of the bed, ready to launch back into the closet. Before she spoke again, she raked back and forth in the large tin once used for a Christmas cake or cookies.

—Of course you never know what possesses Nan.

Listening to her, I thought of hers as a generous idea but a good deal like conceptual art. If Franny had wanted me to have it, she would have left it to me. And Nan would want me to offer *some* remuneration, to offset taxes, which would make it less gift and more transaction. I picked up a flat, opalescent button.

—Blue wool suit, slash pockets, I said.

—God, you're right. I'm looking for a couple of sets to sew on the girls' cardigans.

Jane had always done that kind of thing. I guess she wanted to believe that Livvy still wanted to be included in her efforts. She had used large cookie cutters to remove the crusts from slices of bread, provided cheerful sandwiches in lunch boxes. She hand-painted furniture, sewed Halloween outfits from scratch. Franny used to say Jane had innate creativity. I had innate quirkiness, and Nan, who seldom got her way in anything, was deemed to be thrifty.

Jane circled back to the estate with a few questions about how to divide particular items with her sister. Then she said she was getting us something to drink. She got up and the bed became a seesaw lifting me up and I felt myself drop, though I don't think it actually moved. Franny had believed in a high number of inner coils.

Jane returned with a bottle of Bombay Sapphire and a bottle of tonic.

—Grab some glasses from the bathroom, she said.

She had her rituals and seemed to drink more when we were at the house, as we all did. Jane cut the lime on Franny's dressing table. Later, when I got up, I would see the marks in the veneer. I didn't tell her this hurt to see.

—Mike wants to have that party tonight.

—He told me.

Jane sat down on the bed again. For a moment, I thought she was going to take my hand but she didn't. When we were young and went past a cemetery in the back of Franny's car, it was: *Hold your breath, hold a button, or hold your friend's hand.* Neither my mother nor my father replaced missing buttons, so Jane saved me from oxygen deprivation.

—It's not very blue, this Bombay Sapphire. I think I need a little more.

—They should make the gin as blue as the bottle, I said.

I held out my glass and the gin tipped too quickly in

Jane's hands and some of it spilled out onto the bed. She shrugged and proceeded to fill her own glass to the top and tried to steady it while she sipped. We both began to un-coil a little.

—She kept everything, I said.

—All sorts of crap.

—I think she got worse with age.

—If you find my dad's old letters, it's okay to say. I'd rather know.

—I haven't found anything like that.

Jane picked up a scoop of buttons and let them drop and bounce on the bed, some of them rolling and spilling onto the floor. It was easy to see Franny, her sewing basket next to her, the red cloth strawberry that held the needles and pins, the mixed drink by her bedside table, looking for the right match. I knew there had been a note but thought it had been destroyed years ago. Jane was only six when he died.

—He had fine, small lettering. He never wrote in cur-sive.

—Of course I'll let you know.

She moved her head slightly and took my hand, direct-ing it over her forehead until she had me touching the eye-brow with the scar. I used to imagine there was a big mystery to that scar: that it had been a self-inflicted wound, that Nan had been up to no good, that her mother had hit her. But it had actually come out of roughhousing with her father. He had held her by an arm and a leg and whirled her in their front yard, spinning so hard she became a soundless airplane. She told me they did that kind of thing. She was lucky, Franny used to say. Lucky she didn't lose her eyesight. There was plenty of lawn but he had kicked up a rock in the grass with his foot. A freak thing.

—Franny wanted me to see a plastic surgeon.

Jane kissed me on the cheek. A couple of small kisses, the way her husband sometimes did. And then she lay down and pulled up the covers and closed her eyes.

—Mike and I have been talking lately. You know, about the big picture. I think we're going to be all right, she said.

—Of course you're all right, I said. Then she dropped the topic, said she needed to take a nap before the party.

Trader lay curled next to Mike's chair, no longer woozy from his overdose. The ocean washed under the boards of the deck. The next-door neighbors had come over for dinner. Louise and Tom had a teenaged boy, Taylor, who avoided conversation in a way that Livvy had adopted. I sometimes thought of that family as a pony pack of soda when all you wanted was a single can. I had no troubles with Taylor.

Upstairs there was a pulsing television glow accompanied by droning music. Lights were on in some of the neighboring houses. You could make out occasional laughter down the beach, a bonfire. Tom adjusted his butcher's apron and asked if we wanted anything from the kitchen. He was a man who wore barbecue paraphernalia, funny hats, carried big tongs, even at other people's parties.

—Check on the girls, Louise said. They're sacked out in the clock room. Taylor's in Franny's. As we can *all* hear.

Jane felt around the top of her head, suddenly aware that her sunglasses were fixed there. It was her habit to finish up her days on the beach slowly, in pieces, often waiting until late at night to wash the salt from her body. She stepped into the house and reappeared moments later holding a blue plate with a melting chocolate mousse no one had thought to refrigerate. It came to rest in the middle of the table, where it remained unmolested.

—You leave a boyfriend behind in Chicago, Mattie? Louise asked.

I shrugged and got up to reach the open bottle of red. Mike took it out of my hand and poured for me. I watched the smoke from the citronella candles shift toward us. I shut my eyes until it changed direction.

Louise picked the last of the pink meat from around the salmon bones and shimmering skin. I wasn't sure if anyone noticed that Mike slid his fingers over mine when he handed me the glass or what that meant, if anything. A small electric current ran up my arm. I think it found one of my aortas or ventricles, some place in the odd construction of the heart.

Jane got up from the table. She boosted herself onto the railing and began to swing her feet back and forth.

Mike pulled a chair up for me, close to his, and I sat down. I didn't want to be the small prize in the arcade but I wasn't going to squirm to get away.

Back on the deck, Tom asked:

—What did I miss?

He cleared the empty bottles into a wooden box on the deck.

—Mattie's going to tell us about her boyfriend, Jane said.

She looked almost comical, leaning back, cigarette in one hand, glass in the other, balanced on the railing. She showed none of the cares that would have destroyed my face long ago. She never wore hats against the sun as I do, and she didn't break out at the sight of facial cream. It was as if her skin had been poured out in a dish and put on a level shelf to set.

—His name is Clark, she said, focusing her attention on Mike. He's a short venture capitalist who wears black everything: ties, shirts, suits, belts. Not black with subtle diamond patterns or black with racing cars. Just plain, solid black.

The air turned to a quiet citronella hell.

—Sometimes dark gray, I said, and gave her a look to back off.

—He knows how to mix dozens of tropical drinks, and he has a passion for TV shows on extreme sports, Jane added.

At that point Clark had been the most satisfying sex I'd ever known, which made for a difficult relationship: we had nothing in common. But I had had an immediate physical attraction to him when he'd come to one of the auctions. He was a man who went in for the bellicose—the bronze sculpture of a cockfight, medieval weapons, dis-abled hand grenades. Clark's apartment was filled with that kind of dreck. We'd see each other for a while, then one of us would crave something more or something less. We'd gone on for three years that way, with plenty of lean peri-ods and other relationships in between. My two best friends in town kind of liked him, though they both saw the dead end. For the most part, I had been content to fill and level with Clark. I pictured him back in his apartment in Chicago, wearing only black boxers, sunk into one of his black leather chairs, a hollowed-out pineapple brim-ming with pink-colored alcohol in one hand, the remote control in the other, the phone cradled against one shoul-der. I did not want to discuss Clark Neuhaus.

Mike got up and whispered something to Jane. What-ever he said seemed to prompt her to crush out her ciga-rette and jump down from the railing. She adjusted her yellow bathing suit downward in the back. I watched everyone's attention to this procedure.

Jane searched the cold water of the cooler as if she were hunting fish with her bare hands. She pulled a dripping bottle of chardonnay out of the water and thunked it on the table. Then she wedged in the corkscrew and pulled. The cork snapped in two, half of it lodged in the bottle's neck. Ignoring Mike's offer of help, Jane took a knife and proceeded to ram the cork into the bottle, where it floated.

—It makes me sick to think you're selling the house, Louise said.

Why she thought this was a good approach to changing the subject, I'll never know. But I wasn't tracking her consumption of wine any more than my own. I focused on the lights from the hotel projected onto the water.

—We don't want strangers living here, Tom said.

—We've thought about buying Nan out, Jane said, looking into the living room.

During the silence that followed, a couple of lights went out in the hotel's oceanside rooms. The watery stage broke into fragments.

—Do you have any idea how much this house will go for on the open market? Mike asked Louise.

—I can tell you how much they got for the brown house at the end—the one with the carved fish on the front, Louise began.

—Spare me, Jane said, and poured her glass of wine. She stared at the bits of cork floating on the surface, then signaled for me to join her in the house.

We all felt defeated by Franny's death, the IRS, Nan, natural occurrence, but it's possible Jane took these things harder than anyone.

Jane and I went through the living room and upstairs. Mike remained with the neighbors on the deck. Someone had to. I stopped her in the hall.

—That wasn't necessary, that whole thing about Clark.

—You're not in a very cheery mood.

I wanted to go back downstairs but I worried when Jane got like that. So I let what I could go, and followed her into Franny's bedroom. Taylor and Livvy were there on the bed, and didn't bother to turn from the television. They were watching something called *La Femme Fatale,* the kind of thing you could jump into at any point—staged sex and brutality like time-release meds. Taylor was a large, fuzzy-headed boy who sat slumped over, eating prepackaged pound cake from an aluminum pan. Crumbs dotted the coverlet and floor by his feet. Livvy lay on her belly near the rain of food. I realized that she had a tattoo around one ankle.

Jane led me to the bathroom. She stood in front of Franny's celebrated bubble-bath collection.

—You count the ones on the top four shelves; I'll take the rest, she said.

—Count them? I said.

—I never did that before, did you?

I couldn't think of a time when I had. Her asking made me wonder why not. Some bottles were colored glass; others were clear, with dyed soap. There were dolphin shapes, sailboats, mermaids, and starfish that must have come from an Avon catalog—Franny's shrine to kitsch.

—Twenty-nine on my half.

—Plus thirty-five. What the fuck, she said. Jane pushed her beach hair away from her face and I watched it fall back again. I wasn't sure what she wanted me to say: *Even the best collector can lose sight of her purpose?*

—All poised for Armageddon. I mean, what do you do with sixty-something bottles of bubble bath? Most of them have been opened. Can't you see her trying each one out, just once, a few drops so she wouldn't lose the effect of the full bottles?

—Maybe it was Nan.

But Nan seldom came out to Franny's.

—I've thought about giving them to a women's shelter, but who can trust an open bottle of anything these days?

—Is there something going on with you and Mike?

—We're fine. We're always fine.

I watched her gather an armload of the bottles and as she did, a couple of them slipped from her grasp. They bounced on the carpet, just shy of the tile floor, and clicked together without breaking. I knew instinctively to follow her. One of my bottles tipped in my hands; iridescent blue droplets soaked into my shorts and ran down one leg. Jane cut a swath between the kids and the TV and we went onto Franny's upper deck, which was built directly over the lower one. It was high tide and the beach had disappeared. Jane uncapped the first bottle shaped like an antic shark, and poured the contents into the sea. I followed with the innards of an octopus. From down below we heard Mike shout:

—What are you doing?

I know he would have preferred to be upstairs with the rebel crew.

Jane inspected her fingernails, as if he were caught under a cuticle.

I didn't think I could make an intelligible answer.

—Nothing! she called back.

It wasn't a spectacular display, but there was something satisfying about the sudsy action of the waves. We rushed back and got a second round of bottles. Taylor arrested his television fix long enough to come out and say:

—Cool.

Livvy continued to watch TV.

Soon we were out of bubble bath. We sat on Franny's deck and watched the foam spread out. Jane held on to the railings with both hands, and pushed the soles of her feet against them until her back bowed. I knew she was disappointed, like a child at a bad fireworks display. Her face lit and darkened in the TV light and she relaxed a little, loosening her grip on the deck railings. She crossed her legs yoga-style and looked glumly at the ocean.

—I wish I had my own auction business, I said.

—You always say that.

—My head won't stop humming. Is your head humming? I asked.

—I don't get what we're supposed to do with all of this.

Then she shrugged and turned to look at the kids, the television.

—I can't watch that stuff, she said.

Jane rattled a box of wooden matches, selected one, and scraped the match against the floor of the deck, lit a menthol cigarette.

—If we had had kids at the same time . . . , she said.

She tossed the match overboard. The air had picked up

and was coming directly at us from the islands now. I watched the flag of Jane's hair. There was no one to restrain her once she got going.

—Listen, about Clark . . . or anyone I date . . . I tell you things in confidence.

—You think I'm like my mother? Livvy said something like that the other day.

—No.

It was hard to find a flattering word to say about Jane's mother: her longest-standing relationship had been with prescription drugs and their overlimits. Jane and Nan had been left to nannies and the scrutiny of bachelor-types: all the boyfriends.

Jane made a gesture, like shooting a hypodermic needle into a vein. She didn't exactly laugh. I tried lying down on the deck but it made me feel worse, so I sat up again.

—I live for my girls, she said.

—I know.

Then she pulled herself to a standing position and was down the stairs before I could hoist myself up.

I sat on the chaise in the bedroom and asked Taylor for some of the pound cake. He reached into the new tin he had just opened and pulled off a hunk, handing it to me. His hands were dirty.

—You don't have tattoos, do you, Taylor?

Livvy smiled.

—A couple, he said, his eyes fixed on the kicks and jabs

of *La Femme Fatale*. She flew into her enemy, a tall, athletic man with a black leather vest and no shirt.

—I don't imagine this is a very romantic age, is it?

—Huh?

—You know, romance. That thing that disappoints. It's more virtual now, right?

—It's real TV, Livvy said. She turned her head partway toward me but kept one eye on the tube.

—Exactly. Real TV, I said, watching the man bleed into the floor while La Femme sped off in a black sports car.

—What kind of car is that?

—A Ferrari, Taylor said.

—Aren't Ferraris kind of romantic? I always thought they were.

—They're fucking beautiful machines, he said.

I got up from the bed and drifted over to Franny's walk-in closet. I closed the door behind me. It smelled of cedar and Chanel No. 5. I touched the silks and felt the plastic bags that covered the dry-cleaned items. A faint glow came in under the door and lit the edge of the carpeting. But I knew where everything was even in total darkness. I reached for Franny's sweaters stacked on shelves against the back wall. I was certain they were still organized by color. I made them into a bed and found a couple of shawls to use for a cover. I nestled in but I was unable to quiet the hum.

I thought about the lean, successful men Jane might have had, the charming traders and sailors and pirates, the responsible fellows who bought their homes early and held out enough for a decent golf club membership, the scavengers and bottom-feeders, the geniuses who tormented and smoked and drank themselves to death, the men who built clever things with their hands, the addicts and bad boys, the ones bearing flowers, the pals—all the pals with the ready theater tickets and drugs, the bullies and tyrants, the men who played you with their eyes, reached for you in the dark, called you remarkable or never called at all. And I thought about Mike, and how he'd won out over the rest.

eight

Hole sixteen, the T-Rex. Jane had been gone for two days. Santa Ana winds worked the mini-golf. I was killing time in the shrimpy bathroom, watching Mike and the girls through the loose binding of the door. No mirror, out of toilet paper, bright white walls.

I worked as a motel maid for a couple of months when I was twenty. The owner taught me a thing or two about cleaning products and she said she had one of the first motels in North America to install an automatic device in the bathrooms that periodically discharged a cloud of antiseptic scent into the air. I would be scrubbing away with a plastic-handled brush, a tray of bottled chemicals at my side, when an alpine mist would suddenly drift over my hair like a fine web. I was caught there until Franny found me a job in an auction house.

While Mike and the girls inched around the dinosaur's tail, I rummaged in my purse for a Tampax and latched instead onto one of Mona's fat felt-tip pens. I removed the pink cap and considered the wall. I was not the type to write *Beaver Fever* on the side of a bridge or bomb *Lone*

Kiss on a subway car. Maybe it was the swerve of events. I found myself drawing a cock deserving of a bathroom wall, and inside the shaft I wrote: M and M.

I don't know why I was designed to move around magnetic people. They always threw me. I recognized the risk in orbiting.

The toilet flushed automatically and an unwelcome grace of molecules showered my bare legs. I caught up with Mike as they approached the worst hole, the windmill. The vanes moved in the hot, inflated air. I watched Livvy's springy hair shift about in the currents, her efforts to keep it out of her face as she set her ball on the tee. The object: to get the ball through the sails by way of flawless timing.

Livvy was driven insane by small things that afternoon. The tees, the stupid obstacles. She had gone through fifteen different clubs to find the right one. But it wasn't hard to be patient with Livvy because I could see her struggling.

A teenage couple waited on a concrete bench at the perimeter of the windmill hole. The girl baking in her boyfriend's lap, his baseball cap shading his impatience. I watched Mike adjust the f-stop on his camera. He was the one who had suggested miniature golf. He had a fixation on aging sites, old amusement parks, concessions. He had shot two rolls of thirty-six already. Looking at the couple on the bench, he drew the cover back; the lens pushed out, further still with the zoom. The girl's blank little eyes, the thick coat of mascara, the way she clung to her boyfriend's sweaty neck.

In college Mike used to clip wet photos of Jane along a wire in his darkroom and watch them drip. I kept thinking if Jane had been there that day, she would have made the heat and the anxiety of miniature golf seem normal, fun.

Livvy helped Mona with her swing and I was supposed to mark down Livvy's score. Mike inched next to me and whispered:

—You talked in your sleep last night.

—You were down in the living room?

I barely mouthed this, as if it were necessary to look like a ventriloquist.

—I came down to get a glass of milk.

—You should have woken me.

He moved as if he were going to put an arm around my shoulders, seemed to think better of this, then held the camera out and took a picture of us together, the length of a putter's head between us. That place where the nervous energy bounced back and forth. Later I wished I could get that picture developed. We must have looked happy by the windmill.

I suddenly remembered the game and smiled at the people on the bench.

—Why don't we let this couple play through, Livvy?

But I was the only one who hadn't played, which I figured out when I got her look. I put my ball on the tee.

It was the steep approach that made it so asinine. Even if you were a careful golfer and didn't whack at the thing, chances were the ball would get close to the top and then roll backward, past the tee and into a basin of rushing water glutted with pennies. Mona had made a variety of wishes, pitching her father's coins into the swirl.

—This is taking too long, Mona said, and she began to drop the head of her putter into the grass bordering the ramp, lifting it up and dropping it again. Perspiration beaded on her forehead. It was 95 in the shade. The vending machine was out of Orange Crush and Mike had promised her an Icee and a slice of pizza inside the game shack as soon as we were done. We had two holes to go. Livvy had spent time at the Statue of Liberty trying to convince her that you really could get a hole in one with a yellow ball.

—Don't, Mona said when Mike approached her.

—She won't move, Livvy said.

Sometimes you just have to walk up the ramp and pitch the ball between the mill's sails, listen to it fall through the buried tube and pop out on the small green a few steps below.

—Mona, dear, I can't swing if you sit there, I said.

Mike grabbed Mona around the waist, hoisted her into his arms. She was carried upward, her face lightened.

—Are you related to us? Mona asked.

—You know Mattie, Mike said.

—Is Mom coming for pizza?

I searched for the tiny yellow pencil to add up the scores. Mona put her head against her father's chest, I think to hear an amplified answer.

—I need the car keys, Livvy said.

—Dad said we're having pizza!

Mona's eyes swam.

Livvy reassured her about the pizza and took the keys Mike offered. I watched her walk over the hillocks of the mini-golf.

Mike turned in the clubs and we headed into the pizza haze, the electronic games screwing with my ears. I did the ski run and the race car and the motorcycle wipeout with Mona and then told Mike I'd be over by the exit. I stood inside the glass door of the arcade and watched the car for a while, in case Livvy decided to drive off.

The sun visors in Mike's rental warned that airbags kill children. I have no idea how a parent takes the impact of ongoing caution. Jane told me she stopped listening to the news after 9/11, that she didn't want the girls watching that flight as it hit over and over, people dropping out of towers. Her thirst for news had been quelled. Even pleasant news. And it's true, the hose has been on too long, the ground soaked, water table rising to the point where we are floating in our beds at night, counting car bombs and beheadings, health scares and safety violations. New Orleans and we're up in the attics, trying to break through our minds to take it all in. We have to; we can't. Like quantum mechanics: *cat state.*

Postpizza, we went out to the car and Mona climbed into the back, where she lived with her activity books and Sea World animals. Livvy was allowed to ride up front, being so lengthy. As Mike pulled onto the highway, she fought the glare angling through the windshield with no luck. I watched her withstand the slow action of the air conditioner.

She began to fiddle with the radio. Not just moving from station to station, each one more static-filled than the last, but she made the volume go loud then soft, piercing then quiet. It was a half-hour drive and Mona had fallen asleep at my elbow. I shut my eyes in an effort to let the noise travel through instead of catching and making a migraine with it. If I had allowed that pain, maybe I would have seen what was coming.

Livvy found some blaring rap station and sat back in her seat.

—Turn it down, Livvy, Mike said.

—What? Livvy asked.

In the rearview, Mike looked to have reached his limit. Not with her, I think, but with all the noise. The noise of Jane pulling away. Livvy lowered the volume and faced forward.

Out in the fields, workers stooped to pick broccoli, the trucks lined up, the crates. We were going 70. The smell of fertilizer began to hit the ventilation system. It was crazy to open a window, it only made it worse. Livvy knew that. She rolled hers to the bottom and cranked the volume again.

Later I would blame the heat, the wind, the seating arrangement—the idea that we were supposed to act as a unit, a temporary functional grouping. I blamed Jane. I took it out on myself. I could see the door speaker jumping in its housing. Mike just drove. We were in the middle lane where the asphalt was worn to exposed metal, the tires making their own racket.

—*FUCK!* Livvy shouted and tried to grab the wheel from Mike. I watched the car pull to the right. Maybe I screamed. I'm still not sure. I threw my arm out in front of Mona, and she gripped and pinched it, flying into wakefulness. We sailed onto the gravel shoulder and rushed past a blizzard of ice plant. It hit the windows like brushes in a car wash. We went several hundred feet along the shoulder, stones popping against metal and plastic. Mike's camera flew off the front seat and hit one of Livvy's legs. For a moment I thought the side mirror had broken off and flown into the atmosphere. Maybe a soda can. Mona shouted:

—*No!*

How we missed hitting another car or a tanker I have no idea. Mona began to hyperventilate. Mike got the car into park and clutched Livvy, though the seatbelt pinioned him. She did not try to push away.

—*Mona . . .?* he said. His face was colorless. He shook.

—She's okay, I said and I think I repeated that several times. *She's okay.*

Mona struggled against her belt. Mike reminded her to breathe from her belly. I got her out and Mike reached back and helped her up front. We listened to the engine tick and cool as Mona's breath calmed. Livvy had started to cry.

—What the hell was that? Mike said.

I believe Livvy looked into the ice plant.

—I'm sorry, she said, and took her sister's hand.

—Do you get how serious that was? he said.

—You were starting to nod out.

I hadn't watched Mike every second, so I guess that was possible, in the heat.

—I was wide awake, honey.

—Your eyes were starting to shut.

—Maybe it looked that way with the glare.

—You know what? My vision's fine. I see what's going on. I know what's going on with Mom and . . .

—*Livvy*, Mike said.

—Is Mom coming home? Mona asked, and started to cry as well.

—In a few days, Livvy said. That's what I meant. That I know she'll be home soon. We'll sit in the back together and play dolphins.

—Make sure her seatbelt is good and tight, Mike said.

I moved to one side and the girls climbed over the front seat. Mona nestled on the far side next to her sister and picked up the scorecard. Livvy helped her with the belt.

—You all right? I asked Livvy.

I saw where the camera had left a scratch and raised a bubble of blood just above Livvy's knee. The film had been exposed.

—Sure.

Mike asked if everyone was ready, but he wasn't. No

one questioned his wait. After a while he put on the turn signal and we rejoined the highway.

My mother did most of the driving in my family. But there was one trip that Albert and I took without Lois. I was Livvy's age then and he drove me to the edge of a Civil War battleground. Maybe we were in Virginia.

We didn't get out of the car, though the weather was good, no sign of rain. He didn't talk much, kept his grip on the wheel, his tummy pushed against its lower rim. There were no markers or plaques to be seen. He just understood where the battle had been fought. And all it was, really, was a green sloping meadow, the noise of live bees, the dead bees pressed against the windshield. I sucked at the last of a frosty root beer. Looked out at the thing that was there and not there. The Civil War and the absence of the Civil War.

I wonder what Livvy saw that day.

nine

Mona fell asleep on the way home from miniature golf. Mike carried her in from the car still clutching the score card. He took her up to the clock room and tucked her into the twin bed everyone considered to be hers. Trader followed in their wake. Livvy changed into her striped swimsuit and fixed herself a tuna sandwich. She went out to the deck where she ate and worked on a needlepoint, and appeared as though nothing had happened out on the road. I saw an expression that I nailed as Franny's. That stoic thread.

Mike went out to the deck and shut the French doors behind him. He leaned into the table and they talked. I kept busy, trying to push a migraine away.

Mike often used his hands as if he were building something, but now they were slack. Livvy stopped her work and nodded. I don't know that they settled anything. Maybe there was some easing. A short time later he gave her a kiss on the forehead and they went out for a swim.

Eventually, Mike came inside and Livvy swam out toward the float with Taylor. Mike toweled off. Someone was roofing or paving nearby. The smell of tar filled the living room.

—She'd be a lot better if her friends were around, he said.

Livvy had a therapist back in Boston. Mike told me they'd already talked by phone.

—I don't want to make this about me, but this is probably about me, I said.

—Only if your name is Jane.

—Okay, but I'm not helping.

—Actually, Livvy asked if I thought you'd stay. She wants you here.

—I don't know.

—We just have to stay 6 to 8 inches apart at all times.

—Three miles.

—I'll make it up to you.

I was about to dispute this when the evening commuter rode by and that cabinet door in the kitchen fell ajar. We both looked at the box of baking soda that Jane had opened before she left, and placed on the shelf. I made an effort to tie down my concerns. Mike filled a silver travel mug with coffee. His hands were shaking when he put it on the shelf by the door. He got a clean t-shirt over his head, the word Dollywood across his chest, and found his keys. He had to run errands. A dateline of thought moved across his forehead.

He turned to make sure Livvy wasn't back yet, that Mona wasn't circulating.

—It's like a mudslide, he said. The house inching downhill. Electric and gas lines, the water pipes snapped off.

I handed him his glasses, his wallet.

—So we stay in the house and ride?

—While we can, he said.

I looked at the other things he dropped into his pockets, and something came through my weary conductors.

I had a clear image of Jane. Jane falling through the air. Maybe thrown from a car, or walking off a cliff, or something less ominous. Like a grocery bag filled with old clothes, light silk blouses, scarves, she continued to fall. She was soft and pliable, almost weightless as she dropped. My mind raced to the Golden Gate Bridge. The way people get dressed for those occasions. Her father put on a good suit when he suicided. I knew that kind of thinking didn't help. But Mike kept insisting that Jane simply took off, and I understood the mind's attraction to the poison wish.

The ocean suddenly made me queasy. I never understood how Franny had done it year round, the business of checking for conditions: surf, wind velocity, barometric pressure. It wasn't just about getting the umbrella up or down, it was about those sudden occasions when it was necessary to tie down furniture, tape windows, nail up the plywood.

L ivvy returned from her swim, showered off and went back to the deck and her needlepoint. I wanted to attempt a conversation but I wasn't that secure. I worried she'd run off or accuse me of making her drop her needle between the boards of the deck. And I would be down on my hands and knees trying to find it in the sand. Besides, that boy Taylor had slipped onto the deck fresh from his shower, his damp hair combed back.

They sat around for a while and he drank a soda. She laughed responsively. It was Austenish, weird. I wondered who taught her needlepoint.

When they went back in for a swim, I listened for Livvy's voice in case Taylor was up to no good. I collected the vases from around the house and placed them on the table, playing the game: Ignore the Migraine. I tried to puzzle out Franny's intentions. It wasn't a collection really, more of a wild assortment. There was an unremarkable Favrile that wouldn't fetch as much as Jane hoped, despite the Tiffany name. A Bohemian iridescent that could have gone directly into the give-away bag. Same with the Carter, Stabler and Adams because of the crack at the lip. I assumed Franny did the repair herself.

Nan had claimed the Art Nouveau piece. She had a sentimental attachment to the orange and honey glaze. There were the whimsical majolicas that I like but some consider gaudy. The George Jones would bring a good price. A pair of French Porcelain urn vases had value but I didn't think of Franny as a romantic. Eighteen vases in all—maybe $32,000 to $40,000, a little more if I really worked them. Which meant someone would be dissatisfied. The fight would shift from who got what—

to whether or not I was the one to make such assess-
ments.

I was listening to the crackle in my sore brain, leaning
over the table like a magnifying glass, when I was suddenly
jabbed in the back. I pitched forward and felt Mona throw
herself around my waist, maybe in an effort to catch me.
When I hit the table, the vases went flying. Some chipped,
others shattered, including one of the French porcelains.
The value of its mate plummeted. Four vases remained
standing. I pulled her arms away and turned round.

—I'll make it up to you, she said, her eyes gone to fluid.

She was parroting. I crouched down and asked her how
long she'd been awake. She looked at the bright yellow
bandage on her knees. She was very big on the flexible
sport type. I suggested we sit on the couch and talk.

—I hate all this stuff, she said.

—You know . . . I'm just here to help your folks out a
little, I said.

Mona got up into my lap.

—You can go swimming with me.

—You're a good soul, Mona. But . . . I'm going to have
to lie down for a while.

I explained the word: *migraine.* But she remembered.
Franny often asked one of us to shut the blinds to the deck
when she had her migraines, the sun moving around the
edges of the Levelors. We brought her warm milk and icy
compresses, tiptoed over the carpets. Our toes made impressions we would follow back out of the room.

Mona sprang off and pretty soon she dragged Franny's bedspread down the stairs and across the floor like a firefighter wrestling a live hose. She panted as she draped the bedspread over me. I felt like the big useless doll who talks only when her owner talks her. We had gone round the big questions for now.

I asked her to be a sweetheart and bring me the portable phone. I called the hotel and found someone willing to give me the names of a couple of babysitters off their list. After a few tries, I found a girl named Patty.

She came to the door, an hour later. I wasn't used to dealing with sitters. She had straight wide teeth and made me think of popular girls—the ones who play tennis and golf and never doubt their purpose. Patty took Mona swimming for $25.00 an hour and after I swept the bits of vase into cardboard boxes and paper bags and put them in the hall closet, separated for possible gluing, I dropped off to sleep.

ten

When Jane and I met for the first time on Miramar Beach, I had been sitting on the brittle steps of my parents' new rental, between the deck and the water, thinking about going in. As her skinny shadow covered me, I held onto the iron railing as if a force of nature was about to take me away.

—I bet you don't know the first thing about ghosts, Jane said, closing in.

She pulled up the bottom half of her two-piece suit with a snap. Sand flew from around her waist. I looked at my hands, which were covered in fine bits of black paint from the railing. I didn't understand about showoffs—what makes them do what they do.

—My father's a ghost, she said.

Her hair was stiff and yellow, her bathing suit lavender. Even then she had the small scar across one eyebrow that some men would love.

—Don't you talk? she asked, shifting around.

Beneath its thin coat of paint, the railing was all rusty. The landlord had said over the phone that the house would remind us of something New Orleans-ish. I wanted to wash off, but if I moved, Jane might leave. Just before she showed up, I had been thinking about survival. Lois had spoken to me that morning about going to the Channel Islands. She and Albert, were weather-hard people with soft, wasted centers. They experienced life only when racing sailboats. If the ocean were too treacherous, or windless and flat, they hit the yacht club and loaded up on mixed drinks. Then I was left to my own recklessness, the occasional sitter in tow. We had arrived at Miramar Beach the day before. As my mother talked about the islands, I had scrounged in our carry-on luggage for something to eat. There was no food in the house except airline cookies and peanuts, no plates or silverware, no hand-towel in the bathroom. It would take my mother several days to organize herself for such an effort and then she would take me on a shopping trip that would put grocery bags in our laps, at our sandals, ready to tumble off the ledge of the backseat.

She would apologize, she would talk about her childhood, she would make me regret things that happened to her when she was eight. Then she would center us with a sense of geography. She had screwed her eyes into a local travel guide, and described the three islands we could see from shore; there were eight in all, one completely submerged. She read aloud to me, from the couch in the new living room, about the "lone woman of Ghalas-Hat." An Indian woman named Juana Maria who had grown up on San Nicholas Island. Authorities removed the Native Americans from San Nicholas by frigate, in 1835. Juana

Maria had a baby who was supposed to be carried on board by a friend. But when it was discovered that the baby hadn't made it onto the ship—here my mother paused to imagine the crush of people and events for me—Juana Maria jumped overboard and swam back to the island. For 17 years she remained there without human companionship and never found her child. She came to believe the baby had been taken off by wild dogs.

At that point Lois had stopped and pressed her palm down on my head and suggested a bang trim. Albert placed several bills into my hands. They were all too large, I knew, to break at the coffee shop of the Miramar Hotel. He made me repeat my new address, my full name, the full names of my parents, and the phone number of the yacht club before they took off for the day. Albert often drilled me in a variety of safety procedures, making sure I was disaster ready. He enjoyed listening to police dispatches over the short-wave radio, and talked to me about emergency calls and distress signals. My mother had gone along with this because I could then, she felt, be left safely alone.

So when Jane badgered me about ghosts that day, my concerns were with the Channel Islands. I intended to tell her about the lone woman's baby.

—There's a small ghost out there, I said, pointing out to sea. Jane dismissed my suggestion with a look. You could tell she was full of the world. She told me her name and asked mine.

—Mattie Winokur, I said, brushing my hands together, the paint from the railing clinging fast.

—You haven't even *seen* a ghost, have you, Mattie Winokur?

I noticed a flash of lavender toenail polish as Jane dug her feet into the sand.

—I've seen plenty.

—Where? Name one place.

—The movies.

She worked her feet, using them as scoops. I would learn she had a habit of penetrating situations without reluctance. After a while she held her arms out in front of her like the bride of Frankenstein, as if this were necessary to keep her balance.

—Only certain people see ghosts, she said.

—Do you see any ghosts right now?

I could feel her trying to be patient with me.

—Not really.

She stopped.

—My father shot himself in the head. He was standing at the top of the stairs, and his head rolled all the way down and landed at his feet.

She seemed to search my face for understanding. But then her feet began to move again, driving her downward. Her legs, engines of determination. Finally she lost her balance and I wasn't sure if it was on purpose. She pitched forward and braced herself with her hands. Looking at me, she straightened up and started over, worked her way further into the sand.

It was a chilly June morning, but Jane didn't seem aware of the temperature.

When she fell forward a second time, she hit her face. Sand clung to her in a mask. She sputtered and spat like someone in a comedy show and quickly ran across the slender beach, down to the water, which was maybe fifteen feet from where I sat. She splashed about, making a big act of it. I started to laugh, and I could see this pleased her.

If you watched Jane long enough, you could tell she owned everything there: the beach, the stray black dog that tripped in and out of the surf, the occasional jogger, or piece of driftwood. She returned to me dripping, frozen, no towel.

—Come on, she said, breaking into a jog, looking round to make sure I was following. This was her invitation to the white clapboard house just down the beach, where I would meet the ghost of Jane's father.

But when Jane saw Franny standing by the French doors, she said: He hides when she's around.

—I just bought a cake, Franny called. Invite your friend.

At the dining room table, Nan marked where the slices of chocolate layer cake should be cut. Jane served me first. Franny asked where I lived and how long I had been at the beach. She had a small mole near her mouth which she darkened with eye-liner pencil, a long, narrow nose. Her hair was swept back into a French twist like Sophia Loren.

She gave me a cloth napkin, all the edges and corners lined up, pressed into place. When it sat by my plate too long, she showed me how to unfurl it and place it like a silk scarf over my lap. Nan demonstrated how to hold a fork, what to do if you had to cough at the table. Jane explained the correct way to pour the pitcher of milk, and this became my job. Over time Franny would train us in table manners as if we were to become ambassadors or diplomats. Miniature adults capable of learning anything she saw fit to teach. She would even show me how to remove a foreign object from my mouth so that it would go largely unnoticed. She asked me several questions about my parents. I tried not to make them sound too odd.

—They must be worried about you, she said after a while. Maybe you should check in with them.

She made a gesture so that Nan would mimic and blot the icing from around the corners of her mouth.

I looked at Jane's face. It's possible she was ready for me to go. But my parents were out sailing and I knew, even then, not to appear to be ditched by my clan.

—They know where I am, I said, looking around the room, away from Jane's eyes.

A pile of napkins and tablecloths damp from the refrigerator, waited on the counter by the open ironing board. Franny used to iron her own linen instead of trusting her housekeeper to do it correctly.

After a while, Jane clicked on the radio, and found a jazz station. Franny was big on piano music, she told me. Anything with a strong bass, the right kind of saxophone—nothing brash or shrill. Maybe we listened to Coltrane, I don't know. Bill Evans.

She leaned against the kitchen counter in stocking feet and a straight, sleeveless dress, the jacket off now. She closed her eyes and drew on her cigarette. I imagine she was wearing her jade or the fresh water pearls. A screen of smoke formed in the air, which made her unavailable for a while. Her hips moved slightly. Reaching over, she turned up the music. The ash dropped from her cigarette without her knowing, and she smiled to herself.

Jane and Nan began to bicker in low whispers about who had received the larger slice of cake, and the steam from the iron rose in front of me, heat beading on my forehead. I watched Franny.

—Can I help you iron? I asked.

I think she was amused that I had asked. She wasn't sure that my mother would approve.

—I love to iron, I said.

I don't think that Jane appreciated this gesture. She probably saw it as a small betrayal. Something that would always be there between us. Something to build upon.

I had to wait until I had finished my cake and washed my hands.

Franny introduced me to the seltzer bottle with the cork at the end, all the holes punched into the metal like a tiny watering can. Then she looped the cord through an arm that kept it out of the way when you moved the iron, bending this way and that to accommodate a long reach to the end of the board. She adjusted the board so it was just right for my height and let me set the temperature gauge. Franny had not always had help, and one should know how to do things in a pinch, she explained, as she adjusted the temperature downward. Ironing was a pleasant activity, a way of achieving a quiet state of mind. It was absolute perfection if you took your time and got all the folds right.

I doubt she understood how happy I felt in that moment, listening to her go on about ironing. The sense of importance, the smell of the warm linen. I had never ironed a thing in my life but I pressed everything Franny put before me—sometimes two and three times.

I'm left with unremitting curiosity about what she told Jane, and where she went during those short escapes into cigarettes and jazz. But there's no record of Franny's fleeing thoughts. Nan was too young and I'm sure Franny didn't confide in Jane. Besides, that's not something you tell a child, not if you have any self-control: I mean, that you think of taking off, of giving up, even in your mind, even in a panic.

Of course I knew her differently. For me, Franny produced milk from the palms of her hands. The way gold coins pour from the hands of a Hindu goddess. Stigmata you can spend. I can't explain this mental picture, and I know Jane would not have agreed with my estimation. But that's how Franny appeared to me, and I don't think that will ever change.

eleven

When a neon sign is made, a glass tube is blown and bent into shape. Then it's bombarded by electricity in order to eliminate any dust. The oxygen is vacuumed out and it's filled with gas. Argon puts out a purple light; krypton: silver; helium: pale peach. Neon gas makes orange. I've always preferred the small, homemade signs: *Good Eats, Shoe Repair, Biggie's Pool Hall*. That kind of thing. *Enter. Ladies.*

It's possible Mike put out more light at Franny's than in the real world. But maybe that's like propping two neon lights against a wall. It's not art until someone claims it as Art. I couldn't claim Mike or the voltage he emitted. Anymore than I could cover that kind of light with an old towel or snap it out before I went to sleep. His glass tubes were bent to read: *Find it here.*

Three days after Jane drove off, Patty, the babysitter, came over to play dollhouse with Mona and her rubber people. Mike had negotiated her down to $20.00 an hour. He wasn't raised into money like Jane.

Mike was on the computer and I worked on the silver. Livvy had been bored and finally drifted over to see Taylor. His mother sat on the beach, reading a glossy tabloid inside a copy of *The Atlantic*. Mike and I timed our departures. I left first to talk to some dealers around 11:00. Mike went down to the library to do research at 12:00. We met at the only restaurant downtown with a neon sign. A place for tender grilled fish, the contemplation of nicely-fitting running shorts and sport bras, and the belief that you deserve a table in this idyllic world. The feeling of good health and smart ease all around.

We asked to be seated inside. It looked like rain.

Mike reached past the perspiring water glasses and took my hand, moved my rings around my fingers.

I wanted to ask if things go back to normal when she returns. But that seemed like an Eight Ball question, that almost any answer could float to the surface.

The waiter brought things to the table. I tried to eat some of the bread kept warm by a cloth napkin. The day was cooling off but I felt like a broken coil on a hot plate: cranked up, unable to heat anything properly. I couldn't taste the bread and I had already eaten two slices.

When we left the restaurant, we dashed to his car and inched into traffic. He called the Biltmore Hotel. Before I could say anything, my phone rang and I thought it might be Mona calling to tell me the storm was so bad at Miramar that the house had broken free from its foundation.

—Don't hang up on me this time, Jane said.

Mike's voice overlapped hers.

—Smoking, he said.

—Sorry, I said.

—It's okay, she said.

In that chaotic moment, I was struck by the fact that I missed hearing her voice. She was the one I typically called when I was in a jam. A pocket of my brain imagined a conversation around Mike. Or Livvy. I wanted to tell her I might be learning Mona's rhythms, that I felt sick with guilt.

—Everything okay? Mike asked.

—Patty. She's checking in, I said.

—So Mike's there? Jane said.

—Yes.

—I'll hang up if he gets on.

It doesn't storm much in the summer in Santa Barbara, not in that strictly perfect climate. But I watched large drops of rain suddenly hit the windshield and sheet off the car. A family tried to get their pedal surrey out of the downpour. Their toddler was tucked in the front basket, getting drenched—no effort to haul him in—the quick leg action to make it back to the rental place. They were laughing, crazed with rain. People on roller blades and bikes dashed over the bike path, took off across the park.

—I went bungee jumping, Jane said.

—King size, Mike said.

—Fuck, I whispered.

He put his hand on my knee. The capillaries warmed, tendons crackled. Sometimes he could be deft at dispersing his melancholy, or masking it in a way I couldn't.

I remembered the clear image I'd had of Jane falling

through the air like a bag of light clothes. It had been about stupid risk, nothing else.

Straggler beachgoers fled toward Stearn's Wharf or into cars, ran for the trolley.

—It's changed my life, Mattie. You have to do it, she said.

—Don't worry if Livvy doesn't want to go in swimming, I said. She's been upset lately.

Mike downshifted, turned on the lights. A couple that didn't understand or recognize lightning or shelter moved under one of the tall skinny palms that lined Cabrillo Boulevard. They clung to it as if it were a radio antenna.

—Just tell Patty she's there for Mona, Mike said. Livvy doesn't need a sitter.

—Oh, sure, I said.

—Livvy's upset how?

Jane was at an amusement park. That's what it was. I heard bells. Pops. Little tunes. There was a small one in Santa Cruz, maybe one around the Russian River? I wasn't sure. I could feel the car jerk into motion, heard it crank up the ramp until it reached the top of the park. Full of people, trying to hold on to the rim of the last seat while the roller coaster sailed forward.

—Just watch Mona. She's very easy, I said.

—The view's not that important, Mike said.

—She's just . . . you know, I said.

—You're not worried about her . . . are you?

—Take my watch. It's on the counter in the bathroom. Then you can keep track of the time. No. Mona's . . . big on macaroni and cheese and Livvy might go for a salad if there's enough ranch dressing. And maybe one of those chicken patties in the freezer. They'd probably both like one. You can put them in the toaster oven for about six minutes.

—Stop it. So you're not worried about her?

She had begun to raise her voice.

—For Christ's sake, I said.

I took Mike's hand off my leg.

—Here, I'll talk with her. You finish up the reservation, he said, trying to hand me his phone.

—It's just a bad connection.

I pressed my phone closer to one ear, pushed a finger against the other.

—We'll be in around eight tonight. Can you stay that long? I asked.

—Tell her nine. And with an auto club discount? he asked.

—Where the hell are you? Look, Livvy's . . . stronger than you think. I'll . . .

Then the signal went down, the airwaves blank.

—How about nine? I said into the void.

—Everything's fine, I said once Mike was free.

He said he'd call in a while, just to make sure. The traffic picked up pace and soon we passed the volley ball nets, the Bird Refuge. I made a clear decision what I needed to do was cancel a couple of things back in Chicago. I didn't need cable television, unlimited calling, the bonded and licensed speedy maid service that came once a week and left my bathtub like a receptive womb. I could live without my Vogue subscription. I'd make those calls first thing in the morning. I could economize until I found work again.

I called my message machine. But it was the first time in days. There were no calls from the condominium association. The telephone companies that wanted my business hadn't left messages, just clicks. I was not being head-hunted and if there was a relative out there on a sudden genealogy kick, I hadn't been conceived of yet. In the lobby of the Biltmore, I picked up a newspaper.

Gregory Peck was dead. There had already been a memorial. I stood by a vase of flowers so large it made my spine ache, the thought of arranging it all. I opened up my reading glasses and studied the photos taken at the memorial. Calista Flockhart had been there, dressed in that Audrey Hepburn look. She held a frameless photo of Peck as she stood on the church steps. Maybe it was the memorial pamphlet. My guess was that she clutched his picture to out-gain the paparazzi. Certainly they drove after her on their motorcycles, hoped to run her into a support column or a highway divider. With Greg in hand, she could simply show them his face and go mute.

I wondered if he had ever stayed at the Biltmore. I could see him in the pool: the Coral Casino. I could see him in swim trunks, nothing tight-fitting. Everyone poolside waiting to see if he was going to hit the water, do a few laps, breathe, ask for coleslaw with his sandwich or potato chips.

Mike signed us in, got the key. I told him about Gregory Peck. Mike took this kind of thing seriously. This business of famous people dying. That funny sense that you've lost someone you know. He grabbed my hand and we walked through the lobby, around the restaurant, and outside. No one was playing shuffleboard. The maids' carts full of supplies. The feeling that I should take something, to have plenty on hand.

Mike opened the door to the room and I went off to the bathroom. I was in there a good twenty minutes when he knocked.

—I'm looking for a shoe shine kit.

—You're wearing sandals, Mattie.

—I just want to see if they gave us one.

I cranked open the small window over the toilet, watched the rain drip through the hibiscus bush outside. Cupped my hands to collect the water. I had heard the bathrooms were cramped and dark, no shower-stalls. They must have remodeled. I felt blinded by cheerful tiles and amenities.

—I ordered a bottle of wine.

—Okay.

—You don't have to stay in there.

I wanted to say: *I don't really care about the things we're given, the emergency sewing kits, the free shampoos. I just don't want to lose you.*

Maybe the tiles amplified my thoughts because he pushed the door open then. He looked down at the mound of tissue at my feet.

—I always wanted to stay at the Biltmore, I said.

He took a washcloth and held it under the tap, brushed my hair back, drew warm water over my face. Kissed my forehead.

—She just drives off.

—That's what she does.

—I feel like we're being pulled along behind her.

—Let go?

—Of you?

—No, he said.

—She doesn't call the girls. She hates me and I don't understand why she hates me. I mean now I do of course. I would now. But not then, not when I was trying to get her to stay, when I came out to help. What if she abandons them for good?

—It's about keeping us waiting.

—Great.

—The night my sister died, she was in surgery for hours. After a while, my mother started asking people if we were in the wrong waiting room. She was sure a doctor was looking for us, somewhere in the hospital, that he was ready to tell us she was dead. After a couple of hours, she made my dad and me get up and search the hospital with her. There were eight floors in the hospital and it didn't matter what anyone said. She was convinced they had put us in a hidden waiting room. The one where they can never find you with horrible news. When we rode down to the lobby and she wanted to go to another hospital to look, my father managed to get someone to bring her a tranquilizer.

I took the washcloth from his hands and held it under warm water. I washed his face, his neck. The water ran down into his shirt. I drank the water that ran down his face, the water from his neck. I knew he was a split man. I understood.

The one who held me, that one troubled me, because I knew how much he wanted me. Mike reached for a towel to cradle my head against the floor tiles. My ears rushed with sound, like a steady freeway noise, and for a little while I stopped looking for things.

twelve

I have no affinity for the afterlife. No desire to play with its rolling energy as Jane did. She treated death like a boy inside a tire at the top of a steep road. She stood in his path, unflinching, taunting his friends to let go of the rubber rim.

I've never liked cemeteries. But Jane and I double-dated once at the cemetery where we would later bury Franny. When we were teenagers, Jane had this thing about fixing me up. Sometimes I think she just wanted a group around, but if she made plans for the afternoon or evening, there was typically some guy for me. The friend of the boy she was dating. Or someone she thought of dating but had changed her mind about. Or just a nice guy because she said that's what I needed. An all-weather type. An anorak. I couldn't work out her sense of mete-orology.

She always wanted me to go with her to the volleyball nets at Butterfly Beach, to burger places—sites where boys congregated. Though I was only a couple of inches shorter than she, I felt dwarf-like when they signaled with their barely-fed expressions. And they did, they always signaled to her with their eyes or hips, cigarettes low in their mouths—classic boy stuff.

There were the beach dates. I was offered Cokes and cones from take-out windows for the price of a boy's sandy lotion and sweat. At the far end of the blanket, Jane and her date. She had ease. Her whole body looked relaxed and she kept those guys jumping up and down in the sun. She laughed off anything she didn't want. If she wearied of a boy's attentions, she ran into the ocean. For the movie dates, she convinced me to keep my glasses at my family's rental. In case I wanted to make out, she said. *Otherwise, they'll steam up.* I sometimes thought I could make her happy, even temporarily. We double-dated and knew the back rows of movie theaters. The comedies drove me crazy, especially the physical ones with pratfalls and punches. I think some of those boys considered me sullen or stand-offish, not realizing I was nearsighted. But there were a couple boys I liked in the bunch she procured. I knew they weren't designed for me, but I thought about them later. Tom Rainer came ready-built, for a purpose. And I turned him over in my mind for a while. I don't mean years, but I thought about him. And then, when we buried Franny, the chauffeur we had, he leaned against that exact mausoleum, or one just like the one I remembered, as if there were a circular, repetitive quality to events that we're supposed to get.

. . . . . .

Jane's boyfriend Nate was the one who suggested we go to the cemetery. Maybe he wanted to please her. I was fourteen then, Jane fifteen. I didn't mind going that much, I said. She said it would be like breaking into like a Masonic Lodge or a country club. I had slept over in the clock room, Jane in the other twin bed. We had taken off as soon as Franny began her catlike snore, Nan curled under the bedspread beside her.

Jane told me we would have to climb a wall to get into the cemetery, so I had worn one of my mother's T-shirts meant for boat work. Nate parked on the other side of the rail-crossing. One brake light flinched on its rear bumper, poised to fall. Jane and I ran toward the white exhaust. It billowed from the tail pipe and rose into the street light's beam. She opened the passenger side door. Nate appeared in the front seat like a pop-up ghost in a fun house.

Now he gets too many of Mike's features, his gestures, as I turn up that memory. In the back of the car, Tom, an angular boy with a wide mouth and a pleasant-enough expression. Jane nudged me and I got in the back next to him. I did my best to avoid his long cylindrical legs, one of his feet stretched into my side of the well.

Jane said something to Nate under the scratch of the car radio, then announced:

—Mattie is the smartest person I know.

I felt like getting out of the car. But Tom slid over and

draped an arm over my shoulders, as if he had received a starting signal. I was hot and realized too late, that in my haste to dress, I had forgotten to put on perfume. We drove through the dark, estate-lined roads, crossed the freeway into Summerland and pulled in at The Nugget—a Western place with saddle and bullwhip décor. There were photos above the booths of famous locals who had eaten greasy things at The Nugget. I studied Kirk Douglas's chin on a signed black and white. I wondered if ketchup got caught in the dimple. Attempting to balance a saltshaker in a little pile of salt, I was aware that Tom had inched into my side.

—Do you like staying at the beach? he asked, close to my hair. Nate talked to Jane on the other side of the table that way. I shrugged and Tom laughed as if he knew something about me. I said I was trying to decide between a turkey sandwich and a hamburger. Just then the waitress came up and Tom ordered both meals for me. When the woman went off, he leaned in close. He told me how much he liked my outfit. And how white my teeth were. Maybe he used the line about pearls. I looked at his pants, to see if I could find the bulge of a dating manual. But I was taken in a little.

I dredged my plate for bits of fries, and watched Nate. His voice made me think of the hum of a water cooler, a sound that goes in and out of consciousness. I still couldn't make out what they were saying to one another because Tom kept breaking my concentration. He asked if I wanted another Coke. He asked what my favorite color was. I could see Jane was toying with Nate and it seemed like a wasted emotion. She had told me before we left Franny's that he wasn't the kind of guy you take seriously. He wasn't significant, she said.

But I knew that some people who start out that way can become significant later on and visa versa. I thought about couples all the time then. I watched them just as some people look at a movie to study the lighting or the camera angles. It was a game of determination. I wanted to understand if they fit, if they corresponded somehow, like a pet having similar physical features to its owner. The woman with the pointy nose and her Dachshund, that kind of thing. My father was facially deviant from my mother and that never changed.

Jane caught me staring at her and she did this thing with her eyebrows to indicate that I should look at Tom. But his eyes looked as if he had just received drops to dilate his pupils.

Jane hauled me into the girl's bathroom to say Tom was crazy about me and I said he wasn't, though I might have reddened. We went back to the table with this strange feeling between us. I think Jane finally saw how confused I was and hit a knife against her glass.

—I have a joke about a pilot, she announced.

But Jane's jokes were slow and winding and she often ran them off the road. Then she would laugh and ask if I knew the ending, which I never did. Nate seemed to find all of this endearing. Tom watched me intently. When I made a face, he did too—as if the point of being on a date was to mimic one another. I added more salt to my pile and made a fresh effort to balance the saltshaker. When he asked if he could give it a try, I brushed the salt off the table, some of it flying onto his jeans. He removed the salt with a slow deliberateness.

After we left, we drove through the hills. Tom pinioned me in the backseat as if he were trying to find a door or window to climb in. We parked near the Biltmore and made our approach. At the cemetery, Tom made a step up with his hands, as if this were something he did during break-ins. It took me three tries to make it over. Balancing for a moment at the top, I jumped forward and my tennis shoes hit a flat headstone. Jane and Nate came next, and Tom did a contortion as he landed, like a carpenter's ruler folding in on itself.

We had bourbon not flashlights. I found the flask Nate held out, the glint of silver. Tom took my hand in his over-sized grip. The cloud-cover against the moon like a sheet of waxed paper over a refrigerator light bulb. I would have been curious to find monuments of movie stars, but most of them were in LA.

Natalie Wood is in LA. People leave all sorts of objects near her marker. Marble eggs, tiny quilts, candles, broken 33.3 rpm records.

We walked in the direction of the cliff. Nate was free with his large steps and I had to trot along beside him to keep up. I felt uneasy walking over graves, one indistinguishable from the next.

Jane stopped at that mausoleum, we leaned against the gate and I noted the angels carved above the entry.

—Who can name the world's most famous mausoleum? Tom asked.

No one said anything. I wish I had understood at that moment that he knew as much about burial as Jane did about death and that he intended to press the subject. I could have tried harder to make conversation. He answered his own question.

—The Taj Mahal. All right, try this one. Why would the Neanderthals bind the feet of a corpse together?

Tom moved his hand over the back of my mother's T-shirt, gripping it against my spine.

—I give, Jane said.

—So the corpse doesn't run away? I said as a toss off.

It seemed I was right and, worse, this impressed him.

—There's sending a body out in a boat, he said, his voice building. Death at sea. But exposure . . . that's the one that gets me. Imagine being pitched out in the middle of the tundra.

He squatted down and moved a hand up the inseam of my pants. I probably made an invitation of myself without realizing it, but I found it easy to be with him in some ways. I was aware of his superparts as he leaned into me. That was Jane's name for the male anatomy. She had warned me it might feel like a knife was trying to cut into my zipper.

I'd had my share of bourbon by then, but I recall the significant event. Not how they broke into the mausoleum or how I ended up having sex with Tom off in the grass or how much sex. But I still hear Nate calling my name the

way my mother arrested me out of dreams. I scrambled
to get dressed while Tom complained that his head was
spinning.

—She won't come out, Nate said.

We stood for a moment by the open gate. Tom propped
himself against his friend, trying to catch sight of her in
the dark interior: an accident, a ritualized act, who knows,
something for his list of trivia. I told them to wait.

The space was about the size of Franny's walk-in closet
and I couldn't see a thing at first. I inched along until I
bumped into her with my toes.

—Sorry. You alright?

I crouched down against the damp wall.

—Can you read the names? she asked.

Even when my eyes adjusted, I couldn't make out the
names of the deceased.

—Did I ever tell you my dad's name? David. His name
was David.

It was hard to hear her talk about him, the helplessness
I felt.

—Did something happen with Nate?

—That's a dumb name, isn't it? Nate?

—Kind of dumb, I said.

—Maybe we should have tied his feet together.

—And do what with him?

—No, David. He could never sit still.

She stood up, wavered, maybe she straightened her hair.
I felt clammy and pulled my clothes away from my body. I
hoped Jane would let the subject go.

—Isn't it great that you know which fucking spoons to pick up at dinner now? You can go anywhere without embarrassment. Doesn't that just make your life?

I couldn't tell her what made my life because I didn't know.

—I don't mind that Franny does that stuff, I said.

She got up and took off suddenly. I listened to her bare feet slap against the stones, saw the quick projection of her body outside the mausoleum. Sometimes when I dream about this, she runs out to the cliff. That thought activates one type of dread because I can't catch her in time. In another she has her father's pistol. I picture the ambulance, the travel time to an institution. She's placed in tubs of ice water as her mother was each day for a week when she lost her husband, David. Then there's the one where Jane has Nate's baby out on one of the islands. Or the one I like: she sues her mother for parity. She becomes a household name, a movie star. But the real outcome wasn't that large. And maybe this list was more mine than hers.

I found her walking toward the spot where we had climbed over the wall, as if she were about to propel herself over the top. When I reached out to hold her, she pushed me away. I wanted to do something, but I felt low-voltage, unable to give off light or make a wheel spin.

—Don't ever take her side, about anything.

—Okay, I said.

But it's not as if I could unknot from either of them. She knew that.

I curled into Tom on the ride home, he drove. And

Jane, she let Nate make out with her again in the back seat. I think there was an energy that sometimes went from her father straight to these guys. You could see the trajectory.

That was around the time when Franny started letting her drive the Jaguar sometimes. I don't know why. But Jane typically turned it over to me a few blocks from the house. It was her job to bomb the roads of Montecito with paint-filled balloons. It was my obligation to drive. One night she allowed Nate to sheer off the hood ornament at its base. She regretted this later and tried to get it back from him. I heard the whole conversation, lying on my stomach, next to her on Franny's bed. Franny was out at a dinner party. I ate a navel orange.

Jane covered the receiver with a pillow.

—I'm going to hang up on him. Maybe he'd listen to you, she said. But my hands were sticky so she wouldn't give me the phone and a moment later she returned to his voice. They talked until I fell asleep.

I found the hood ornament in the bushes the next day and gave it to Jane who said: You can't weld it; it won't look the same.

I felt like the accessory and I couldn't look at Franny when she told us the car had been damaged by vandals. I think she knew what had happened. But in that generous way she dealt with us, she simply found a replacement ornament at a salvage place in Goleta, and quickly had it restored.

thirteen

The bony world of Egon Schiele, color plates of Navajo rugs, the light projected by Arthur Rackham. I stretched out on the rug and pulled those books up around me. Livvy went back and forth for sun block, cool drinks, stepping over my legs. On the last trip she had put Trader on a leash to take him outside. The cat tried to shrink and slip backwards out of the noose, but Livvy knew how to soothe him. They settled into the cool below the deck. Mike and Mona were out for the afternoon, so when the doorbell rang, I untangled from image and pushed off the floor. I straightened the short rayon skirt I'd borrowed from Franny's wardrobe, held my hair back with one hand, opened the door with the other.

A woman: white slacks, navy ironed blouse. The look of Blue Willow china. Her sandals were grimeless. Her razor cut came to the edge of her pearl earrings. She smiled as if I were someone on a real crime show she had just identified.

—Jane, this is a marvelous property. I hope you realize we're in a vigorous seller's market, she said, extending her hand.

No one had ever called me Jane before. I should have corrected her, but there was something about goofing with realtors. I quickly realized Jane had made an appointment with this Mary, without telling me. Mary was a top seller at a high-end realty company. I asked her if she'd like a legal pad, some pencils. She showed me her bleached teeth and I let her go. Once she possessed the center of the living room, she turned, runway style.

—I have a couple coming up from LA next week. I'd like to show the house to them.

—And you think it would sell for . . .?

Mary took a quick peek upstairs. Franny's bed had gone unmade, sandy towels worked up a mildew on the bathroom floor, wet bathing suits ringed the drain in the shower. Half empty glasses and cups, open lipsticks: I had no idea how many had found their way upstairs. When she returned, she pronounced a hideously large figure. I knew Nan would insist on a sale.

—Did your grandmother add the upper deck or is it original?

—Mary . . . it is Mary, isn't it?

—I could give you my card. That would help. I did tell you I sold that lovely nautical property just down the beach before it hit the listings, didn't I?

She drew a card from her leather holder. She gave me a list of properties she'd sold in the last year. And pulled out a pad on which she had indicated the minor changes we should make to the home. She had a carpenter, plumber, the best electrician in the area. She would have a florist set potted plants around the outside of the house, daily arrangements inside. A funereal atmosphere, as far as I was concerned. I tossed everything on the coffee table.

—Do you drive a Mercedes or a BMW? I asked.

She pulled her jacket in. Her strappy shoes followed me around the living room. She was eating up a tunnel of energy.

—Sorry. I'm having a little fight with my husband, I said. He's very strong on the BMW but I think . . . why bother?

—I like my Mercedes, but maybe men prefer BMWs.

—Or some men. Some men prefer BMWs. Mine does.

—So you design sets, Jane?

—I'm working on a production of Peter Pan . . . for a Boston theater. About Peter Pan's suicide.

I soothed her impulse to laugh by making the connection to trains and the causal account of Franny's death, a sidebar about an author's willingness to siphon off anyone's life.

—I'm awfully sorry about your grandmother. I lost my father last year.

I watched her haircut sway and fall into place again.

—I brought a list of comparable homes, not that anything is exactly comparable, but this will give you a pretty good idea. I'd like to send a photographer out tomorrow.

She slid a folder my way. I set my coffee cup on top of the heavy embossing.

—Do you think things happen for a purpose, Mary? Even if you can't sort out that purpose at the time?

The coffee ring spread into the folder's vellum. Maybe she wanted to get a clean one out of her briefcase, yet she stirred her sugar and settled in.

—I knew a man who fell in love with his next-door neighbor. This is a true story, I said.

Before she could interrupt, I told Mary the story of two families, the couples and their children get along great. They make barbecue smoke together for five years. Then one day, the wife in house A drops by house B for a stick of something. Butter? Standing in front of the refrigerator, Husband B breaks down and confesses his love for Wife A. She has similar feelings. But instead of running off they suggest a trade to the cuckolds: lover for lover, tool bench for tool bench. It's hard to figure out the mathematics on swapping the kids. They have quite a few, collectively. Husband A and Wife B agree, after some distress, and slide into the vacant master bed together, after a minor altercation over who gets the new quilt and matching pillows. The new families live this way for several years until one of them moves to Toledo to take advantage of a job opportunity.

It's possible Mary found resonance. She told me about her sister who fell madly in love with a man who invented a new way to seal plastic bags. Her explanation was technical in nature. I think it had something to do with the fact that plastic doesn't breathe and we do. I love California. How quickly people open up.

—They have a large wedding and move into his six-bedroom house in Newport, Rhode Island. They go to the jazz festival every year. Anyway, three months after they marry, she discovers that her new husband has a twin.

—Who lives in the attic and sometimes . . . exchanges places with the husband?

—Not exactly.

—Too Gothic?

—She fell in love with both of them and the brother moved in. Is that nutty, or what? Our parents still don't know. Or they know, but they don't acknowledge it.

The art of selling works on alignment. Mary tapped her pen against her wrist. She looked like she was considering shifting my meds.

—I don't know if I mentioned this. But I recently sold a five million-dollar house on Jameson Way. The funny thing is, one of the owners refused to sell her stove. I got her everything she wanted in the deal but she wouldn't budge on that one item. The whole kitchen had been built around the stove and in the end, it probably cost her fifty thousand to keep the five-thousand dollar stove.

We both looked at the nondescript radar range. Franny had talked about replacing it many times.

—What if there isn't another couple to take up the slack, Mary, to neatly swap. What if people get deeply screwed up and things fall apart and no one wants to sell?

—I'm not sure. . . .

—I think . . . I feel the same way about this stove, I said.

—Everything is negotiable.

—I can't sell this house.

I knew my words were corrosive, but I couldn't stop myself.

—Were you thinking of buying a new home in the area?

—I can't sell, Mary.

I tried to follow her strong realty talk. She was, after all, my best friend now. She understood me. She wanted to help in any way possible.

Soon I was walking her out to the alley, steering her, really. I had the nauseating feeling one gets after making an incomplete list of sins. I wanted to clarify the exact problem I was having. But already her Mercedes had bumped over the railroad tracks and disappeared. I stepped out of Jane's skin and waded into the ocean for a swim. She hadn't called in a couple of days and I worried myself in the direction of the islands until I was exhausted and had to swim back.

Maybe the draw was Taylor's new IPod. Or the snacks and drinks he had stashed in a cooler in the sand. That was Mike's assessment of why Livvy showed interest. Taylor's parents were in Arles or maybe Paris by then. He was supposed to be at a camp focused on throwing pottery or scaling rock walls or adapting to a shooting range. I hadn't kept up. Mike had agreed to check in on Taylor but I wasn't sure how you check in on a boy that age.

I did find myself inching toward the French doors. I couldn't get a full view through the slats of the deck. One of them, Livvy or Taylor, manipulated the game. Jagged ribbons of sound arrived. They talked in amplified voices, laughed conspiratorially. Pot wafted upward.

When I was fourteen, like Livvy, I drank beer in a juice glass, tried out my mother's Viceroys, found my father's dirty cards in his top dresser drawer. I never wanted to be fourteen.

—This game sucks, Taylor said.

Livvy responded with a horsy, infatuated laugh.

—You just have to talk nicely to it, she said.

—You really eat those things?

—Yeah, but they give you putrid breath.

—Lemme see.

There was a lull and then Livvy shouted:

—STOP IT!

I propelled myself below deck to find Taylor blowing smoke up Trader's nose. I watched the cat shake his head as if he were trying to get a bug out of his brain.

—Livvy! Taylor! Upstairs! Now!

I was shocked when they obeyed.

I stood there and looked at the towel and body impressions they had left, the soda cans, waxed paper, and empty bottles of sparkling water. Boxes of food and sort-of food.

I recalled what Jane had said on the subject of drugs. Something like: if she ever found out her girls were experimenting with marijuana, she would insist they do it at home. Maybe she believed this or maybe she was quoting from a magazine article. She had said this strategy would minimize spin-off troubles like STDs, pregnancy, car accidents. She had given containment a good deal of thought. A good deal.

They sat on opposite ends of the couch. I looked at Taylor's sand-coated feet on the coffee table. He drank a sweaty Coke, looked at the blank television. Livvy leaned her back against the armrest so she could gaze out.

—You know how to roll? I asked Taylor.

He reached for the remote.

—Leave the TV off.

—Okay, Mrs. Robinson.

—Just roll, Taylor.

—Who's Mrs. Robinson? Livvy asked.

—A suffragist, I said.

Taylor laughed and Livvy tilted her head as if this would create a vertical sight.

On the cover of *Time* was Prince William's face. Taylor assembled a single-paper joint on his glossy image, licked and sealed it. It was so tight it barely drew.

Livvy had a goofy smile now. I guess we all did.

—The guys who grew this shit got busted. Fucking helicopter sweep, Taylor said.

—Have you done this at home before? I asked Livvy and exhaled.

—Works for me, Taylor said.

—With Mom? Are you kidding? Livvy asked.

—So what's up with your mom, anyway? Taylor asked.

I reached into the box on the coffee table and for the first time in fifteen years, I smoked a cigarette, one of the stale Pall Malls. My hands shook. I told Taylor to help himself in the kitchen. But he was already coming back with a dozen chocolate-glazed donuts.

I held a joint in one hand, a cigarette in the other, a donut in my lap. Frosting and grease worked into my shorts. Perhaps Jane would have gone about things differently. Trader batted a bit of donut around. Livvy stood in front of the French doors as if she were expecting someone to come up from the beach, the way I think Jane sometimes anticipated her father's ghost. The light was so overdone all I could see was her black form. I got that her arms were crossed over her chest, her legs slightly apart for ballast.

—Your mother called from an amusement park, I said. Everything's fine. She's fine.

—When? You talked to her? When?

—Last night. I didn't want to say anything around Mona.

—Jesus. She hates amusement parks, Livvy said, her voice flattening out.

I got her a glass of water and a roll of toilet paper just in case. Typically, there were several boxes of Kleenex on hand, but we were out. She spun all the paper onto the floor. I watched it pleat back and forth in a pile at her feet. She handed the empty roll to Taylor and he made a bong.

With a surf ski it's possible to take out a dozen young kids, boys mostly, crowded into the sweet spots, as they sit on their boards. Or to lose focus and drift toward

LA. But I sat, nearly motionless on Livvy's Burton, waiting for a decent set to come through. Taylor and Livvy bobbed in the water nearby.

—Get ready! Livvy yelled.

I paddled the wrong way and the surf ski lifted on a modest wave and eased back into place without forward momentum. Livvy gripped Taylor around the waist and laughed. Then she rested her head against his back.

I relinquished my turn to Livvy, who knew what to do.

Later that day I would go over to the McCulloughs' and make a small purchase from Taylor. It seemed pricey but he pushed the quality factor, the locally grown aspect, the *purity of life*. I did not ask what this phrase meant though I wrote it out on a piece of paper. He reminded me that folks had gone down by helicopter for this pot.

When I got home I found Livvy out of the shower, dropped off on the couch. I went upstairs, touching the wet footprints she'd left.

I had read about shape-shifting. I had not become athletic, or trim and fit. But I had gotten into the water every day and now it dripped from my hair and ran down my chest, over my stomach, a drop poised in my belly button, others nested.

Stripping down in front of the bank of mirrors in the bathroom, I watched the smoke coil, wiped a band of steam away, thought about my breasts.

I wrote: *pure life* in the steam.

It's easy to start things, no problem.

fourteen

For a time we experienced life at an altitude-sick elevation. Like camping in the High Sierra. Mountains and water, the absence of trains. Trees that grow sideways to accommodate hard wind patterns. Sun slanting through clouds, pooling at angles on hillsides. Beautiful but all wrong, exposed, subject to lightning.

I broke down and played Monopoly. Livvy beat us. I did not return the Realtor's calls. Mona introduced me to her dolls—again. When we went to the store, she rode in the shopping cart, which meant crowding groceries around her legs. She was a little old for this, but it wasn't such a bad thing: pleasing her. Mike and Livvy decided we should purchase a variety of ripe cheeses, an overload of unbruised fruit, gummy snakes, Loredos or Toledos, fresh shark, roasted chicken, frozen things. Mike took calls. He smoked more. We all smoked except Mona. Fed Ex arrived with videos for Mike to view. He began to tell the girls stories about Franny.

Mike and I were cool when the girls were around. Of course we went insane. He called me on my cell phone when I was in the tub late one night. It was like a voice-over that slowly shifts into a character on the screen, so that I saw him there, on the edge of the tub. He touched my legs in the soapy water, he leaned down and got wet, then evaporated.

I began to worry that Jane had disappeared entirely. Then she rang one night at dinner and asked to speak to Livvy. I don't know what they said. Livvy pulled the hall phone into the clock room and I helped uncoil the cord, which was fighting her. Livvy shut the door. When she was done, she asked me to get Mona. Sometimes I forgot the noise of the clocks.

Franny used to set the timer on the O'Keefe and Merritt stove if she tried to bake anything. Then Jane got into that timer. Just goofing around at first. She gave herself seven minutes for a bath, three minutes to put dishes away, I believe it was twenty-two to practice the clarinet, which didn't include greasing the cork and aligning the parts, a process that was timed separately. When we watched television, the pixels dissolved promptly even if the show had forty seconds of canned laughter to go.

My guess is that her measuring of time had something to do with the unrestricted way Franny had raised Jane's father, and a sense that if Jane had a little control over things, like time, no one else would disappear. The running and setting of clocks: a way of preventing future unhappiness. She was the one who started the clock collection with a small Mickey Mouse from Disneyland. His arms went round and round, the little gloved hands. And then I think Franny kept it going to please Jane.

It's possible Jane really felt we functioned better if we had to stop and realize it was two P.M., and I was sent to my parents' rental to wait out the afternoon naps and lessons and dinner and dessert and silent reading and the filling out of personal charts before I was allowed back for an hour, sometimes an hour and a half or even two.

I was glad when she moved out of that phase.

Over the next few days, I watched Livvy warm, recoil, open, shut. We shifted from a chronic diet of takeout to home-built salads and back again. One day I think all I consumed was a Coke and a basket of fries. Taylor hung out a little, required larger orders of pizza. Livvy beat him at War. We went to the Natural History Museum, and I was surprised when Livvy came on these outings. Mona pressed the button to move the rattlesnake's tail. I read about jellyfish. When they sting a human being, the long spear-like hook pierces the skin, then the surface of the spear fans out into many hooks, which anchor in the body.

Livvy took her sister's hand so she could view the medicine man in the large glass case, a shaman made of wax that would not melt as long as the temperature was properly maintained. I wondered if Livvy knew. If she had sussed us out. But she didn't say and I didn't really think so. Mike and I looked for containers with tight lids to store guilt. We talked about collusion, a state of temporary being. We couldn't see where we were headed.

But there was an ongoing sense of slippage. The total compression of time, from her departure in the Jaguar? Nine days?

We asked Patty back. I admired her flawless disposition. Mona liked having a big person to herself.

Mike and I met at a different hotel, up in the hills where it's possible to sight a cougar if you're lucky, roadrunners, coyotes. Information posted in the lobby about the fauna. Urgings not to feed them.

Out in the heavy smells of chaparral, we made out against the door to the room. I *tried* to get the thin plastic key into the slot so we could make it inside. I looked for green lights.

I wasn't aware at first that a man stood a couple of doors down, watching us, until he sent a loud intentional throat-clearing into the air. I think he was wearing something that marked him as a tourist. Maybe he was an angry Rotarian who didn't believe in this kind of love. Even in a blur, without my glasses, I could see the bad look. I carefully pulled Mike's head up. I pulled my bra cups back over my breasts, lowered my t-shirt.

Mike zipped up and smiled at the man, saying:

—We're here for the wildlife.

I got that card to work.

We cracked up about his face, his jacket. Then Mike loaded a glass with ice as I stripped the bed to its sheets. He made me a gin and tonic. He asked me to lie down and close my eyes.

He placed the glass in one of my hands.

—Can you hear the sound of the ice knocking against the glass? he asked.

—Is this a koan? I said.

—Yes. Close your eyes again.

—Then, no. I can't.

With my eyes shut, he began to undress me.

—You will, he said.

—I'll hear the ice?

—Yes.

I didn't spill a drop until the end.

When we woke up I smelled the gin and lime in the sheets, saw the glass with the melted ice sweating into the bedside table, the pillows on the rug. I pulled the top sheet over us, AC cranking to little effect. He whispered against the crown of my head. I could feel the sound move down my spine into my sacrum. It was something about things being all right.

—I'm glad Franny isn't around to see how we've come undone, I said.

—Jane would never have left with Franny around.

I told him what Jane had said, the morning she left: about him marrying me if something happened to her.

—That was the champagne they served at cousin Linda's wedding in the Berkshires.

—Okay, champagne. But what did you say?

—I assured her that nothing would happen to her. Three hours later, I told her, all right, if she died and if you were available . . .

—I imagine that went over well.

—It's one long line of unravel.

—I don't think I ever gave her reason to worry in the past, do you? And I have . . . had . . . have a decent life in Chicago, minding my own business.

—With good old Clark?

—Stop.

—You still see him, don't you?

—Not really.

—But sometimes.

—Sometimes I wish I could get my intuition to work on demand.

I looked at the clock. Only a little time left, a short afternoon in a hotel that forced things, chopped our conversation apart, then an effort to stitch things together, enough to reenter Franny's house with a good face. We showered and dressed and got in the car. He said I was not to worry. I think both of us would have liked that kind of determination.

—If you'd seen this coming? he asked.

—I don't know.

On the drive back, I asked about Livvy. He said he talked with her therapist daily now, by phone. That Livvy really did seem to think he had nodded out in the car that day. That she was feeling a widening strain over Jane's departure.

. . . . . .

Hotels.
I ate the mints off his pillows, he fretted openly about my leaving. I hid my panic in a variety of bathrooms, looked at the names on fixtures. I let Franny's estate slide.

fifteen

We went onto the deck, through the house, and up to Franny's bedroom. I had only known Jane a week then, but we spent all our time together. She said we were going to surprise her father. Though I didn't believe his ghost was there, I went along. Jane put on her grandmother's red slip over her bathing suit. She gave me a fire-green Chinese jacket, Japanese shoes that tipped forward or backward when I walked, and a wide-brimmed hat choking with artificial chrysanthemums. Jane did our eyes dark enough to vanish, our lips to match her slip. Our cheeks smoldered. She didn't want to bother with her little sister, but Nan wouldn't leave us alone.

—Put lipstick on my eyebrows. Pink lipstick, Nan said.

—You don't put lipstick on your eyebrows, you use eyebrow pencil, said Jane. She propped her sister on Franny's chaise. Jane sharpened the pencil with a tiny sharpener, the coil of trimmings dropping into Nan's open hands.

—Now sit still.

But Nan didn't want to sit still. In her efforts to get away from the pencil, she knocked over a vase by the side of the chaise. It was a rare art deco vase, one of Franny's favorites, as it happened, and now it had a bad chip in it. Jane put Pink Nuance in a great arc over her sister's eyebrows like a clown, twisting the lipstick up to the top. After the first application, it snapped in two. Then Nan wanted to wear Franny's tallest heels, a pair with white sequins, but Jane made it clear that *she* would wear them.

Nan didn't seem to follow much of this, and I'm not sure I did. Midway through Jane's explanation, her sister decided to take off all her clothes, insisting on dressing up with us. When she was ignored, she picked up the phone by the side of the bed and eyed the phone number on the pad of paper.

—I'm going to call Franny, she said.

—Stop it! Jane said, taking the receiver from her hands and resting it in its cradle.

—Franny said you have to play with me.

They *did not, did too* until Jane put a sheer white blouse on her sister, along with a linen apron. Nan was to be the maid.

—Her bottom's showing, I said, without realizing this meant I was taking Nan's side.

—Don't be ridiculous, Jane said. I have tons of fashion magazines.

We watched Nan turn in front of the mirror of Franny's dressing table. She went round and round, chasing her apron strings and regarding her naked behind, content with the world. Grabbing her midflight, Jane pushed Nan's silky hair away from one of her ears and whispered fiercely. Nan ran off to the spare bedroom, where the two of them stayed in the summers. There was only a handful of clocks then, each one set at a slightly different time. Nan returned, holding the apron up around her waist, proudly displaying a new pair of underpants with the word SUNDAY emblazoned on the front.

—Where's your grandmother? I asked.

—Off hunting, Jane said.

I didn't know then that she meant for antiques. But I knew Santa Barbara was a good place to hunt down actors. My mother said that all sorts of stars lived in the surrounding neighborhood or came through for the summer months, and that we shouldn't be surprised to run into some of them on the beach at Miramar. She bought me a feather-topped pen and an autograph hound that I asked everyone to sign. Grocery clerks, waitresses, delivery guys. They covered the ears, the tail, the snout. There was an actor who signed between the legs. He starred in a TV show about tiny people on a big planet.

Franny did have a housekeeper named Trudy but I don't think she realized that Trudy would do anything to avoid watching the girls. Sometimes when Franny went off, she would walk down the beach and visit with a friend who worked at another household. I don't know where Trudy was that day. I doubt her presence would have helped matters.

—Bet she'll be mad, I said, looking over at the dressing

table. It was carved in a deep yellow bird's-eye maple and held a beveled mirror (over which Jane and Nan would fight someday). There was the riot of makeup on the glass top, the damaged vase. Face powder sprinkled like flour from a mad baking session. I don't know how many lipsticks broken in two.

—Don't be a small thinker, Jane said, adjusting a strap on her slip.

—Well, if . . ., I began.

—Shhh. You're stirring up my father.

—You're stirring up our father, Nan said.

Jane indicated the tunnel of dry-cleaning bags hanging in Franny's closet. I could live a thousand years and would still swear those bags began to move, as if on command— the disembodied spirits of the Royal Road Cleaners. I watched Jane shift in Franny's heels, trying to keep her ankles from turning in. Suddenly she drew herself up, holding a silver hairbrush high in the air. All the bags ceased to move. Jane stepped into the long cemetery of a closet and disappeared.

Nan flopped down on Franny's Oriental rug, the one with the Chinese pheasants that swooped from one end of the room to the other, as if she was used to waiting there for Jane. She watched with cow eyes, pleased, I think, to be with the big girls in any capacity. I tried to sit on the edge of Franny's bed but kept slipping off the satin coverlet. Nan rolled her eyes.

Even though I knew it was a game about her father and all, my heart worked when Jane called me to join her. I let her think I believed in those little tricks. The idea of it, that I would go along with anything, as if I was hers for the taking, was a pleasant thing for Jane.

The light blazed from the ceiling fixtures in the closet. The plastic bags grabbed at my arms and drew against my head. My hair, filled with static, danced upward. Despite a watertight belief system that rejected ghosts, my breath was uncontrollably loud.

—You look funny, Jane said, pointing at my head.

—You do too, I said.

—She won't follow us in here, Jane said.

With her hands, she calmed the electricity on her head.

It was true. Nan stayed outside the boundaries of Jane's sanctuary as if trained to do so.

Jane slipped past me and closed the door. I became aware of the smells of cedar and suntan lotion. She took my hand, and we sat near the folded sweaters, thousands of them: pullovers, cardigans, and wraps, stacked to the ceiling. The angoras on the bottom were mostly the colors of sherbet.

She reached under a row of shelves and pulled out a bag of peanuts, roasted and salted in the shell. We took turns fishing for the whole ones, cracking them open with our teeth and nails. I had forgotten how starved I was.

A sudden scratching noise on the door made me jump, but Jane only looked irritated. This was followed by a long whimper from outside the closet.

—Ignore her, she said.

I studied Jane's face and eyed the light switch. I was

poised for events: unnatural occurrences, the headless father. And I didn't like the idea of someone who lingers. When you die, you die. No inching back, no second-guessing. No asking someone to hold your place, the sweater on the back of the movie-theater seat.

—Don't worry about my dad, she said, as if she were tracking my thoughts. He only comes when I'm alone. Anyway, he's all put back together now. They do that: put you back together after you die.

—How?

—They stitched his head back on his body with a real needle and thread. And I think one of his ears fell off too, so they had to stitch that back on so he can still hear me. We talk a lot. But you can't see the stitches or anything. They did a really good job.

—I saw a movie where they sewed a man's head onto someone else's body, I said.

She assured me this hadn't happened to her father. But we were interrupted by Nan's voice against the door.

—I peed in my pants!

—Go sit in the tub and wait for me! Jane shouted back.

—I can't walk!

—Then sit down on the rug and wait!

There was a short, teetering moment before Nan whined:

—My legs are stinging!

—Take a shower! Jane said.

—The handles are too high!

—For Christ's sake, Nan, get in the tub and turn the water on!

Before long we heard water running. I continued to watch for sudden movements among the hatboxes and the shoes. Many of the shoes were in fabric, with beading to match a variety of outfits. There were soft leather boots that felt like whipped butter or frothy cream. I breathed in Franny's colors. After a time, I couldn't tell if I was listening to the surf from the open balcony off Franny's bedroom or if Nan's water was still running. I wanted to say something. But I didn't want to second-guess Jane.

Jane told me about her mother. She was always exhausted and had begun to date a man who ate lemon candy because his breath smelled bad. Jane would stand as far from him as possible whenever he came over. But her mother was always taking her hand, bringing her in close as if the boyfriend and Jane were intended as gifts, one to the other. They lived in an apartment, not a house, but she had her own bedroom and a white phone.

—Let's go out on your boat, Jane said.

My parents rarely took me out. They were gypsies who followed weather patterns, wind conditions, gold and silver cups and bowls and placards, cutting boards and cheese knives etched with dates and names of races.

—It's new . . . and a boat has to . . . settle, I said.

She gave me a compassionate face. I watched her scar change as her eyebrows rose. It appeared almost like a question mark.

—Is your sister okay?

—She's does that all the time. I can show you how to catch a ghost if you find one at your new house. But it's kind of messy, so maybe we should do it another day. But I can show you one I caught.

She pushed some of the longer gowns aside and reached behind several boxes of shoes. Apparently she had stored a large inventory of treasures beneath the shelving system of Franny's closet. She retrieved a full bottle of Chanel No. 5.

—It's really hard to catch them, she said.

She pointed to what looked like a tiny bead or pearl in the bottom of the bottle—probably something from one of Franny's shoes. I pushed my glasses up on my head as if this would help me study the object better. Sometimes I preferred not wearing my glasses. I liked the comfortable blur. But I didn't need proof. Jane had put something in that bottle from the place where her father was trapped.

But she didn't have a chance to show me much about spirit manipulation. We heard a scream just then that seemed to start at one end of my life and go all the way through to the other.

Jane and I rushed to our feet, knocking heads as we rose. The bottle of Chanel No. 5 flew from her hands. In slow motion I saw it hit a closet bar holding a row of blouses, the stopper breaking free. The scent of Princess Grace cascaded, showered every piece of silk, the rayons, the new mink coat, the fabric shoes, and all the suits.

I got the closet door open first, and we saw water spreading out into Franny's room from her bathroom. A voice followed in its wake:

—Jane!

If time winds slowly forward, it also snaps back and breaks. Then the effort to splice it together. I saw Jane go stiff, expressionless. Shock, disassociation, whatever you call it. She must have believed that her sister had drowned. She appeared too frightened to find out. I ran over and saw Franny standing in six inches of water, one arm around Nan, who was sopping wet but uninjured. I had a series of stupid thoughts. I was worried that this slender woman in heels was about to lose her balance in that river. I considered that she and Nan were in a movie. Franny was beautiful enough to be a film star. She was dressed for a fancy luncheon or fashion show—a shoot.

We were all underwater then, floating independently, none of us able to reach the others. The raw sunlight. The smell of the ocean from the open windows and doors to the deck mixed with the smell of Chanel No. 5. I looked at Nan's clown makeup streaked across her face. I looked at Jane frozen by the closet. Without taking time to remove her jacket, Franny plunged her arm into the full tub, grabbed the plug, and turned off the thundering tap.

Then a jarring edit and Franny and Nan were holding on to Jane, as if the water might send her over the deck railing. It was one of a half-dozen times I would see Jane cry. When Franny broke free I looked at Nan. That moveable annoyance who had giggled when I slid off the edge of Franny's bed was waiting to see what her grandmother would do to Jane and me.

—Get some towels! Franny shouted, throwing the ones from the towel racks onto the floor.

She didn't mean me, necessarily, but I knew how to bale and dredge and work hard. I wrung out the towels, lifted up rugs and ran them out to the railing of the upper deck to spread them out in the weather, tearing down to the garage for a mop and bucket, leaning my shoulder into the effort.

The rest would be left to Trudy's skills as a cleaning lady—apparently this was where she shone; a surly building contractor who smoked Havana cigars; the Royal Road Dry Cleaners.

We went downstairs and watched Franny remove several paintings before the water seeped down one wall of the living room. She seemed to know the patterns of damage as well as repair. We followed her to the garage, where the water also dripped. She moved the Jaguar out into the lane. We had run out of towels. Franny threw large black garbage bags over the beautiful leather upholstery. She made her calls while Nan went to rummage for a snack in the kitchen and Jane was told to sit at the dining room table and wait. Franny didn't say it meanly, the way you might think. Jane sat straight in the Stickley chairs. She drummed her toes lightly against the supports of the dining room table until Franny sat next to her and put a hand on her leg so Jane would stop.

—I have something to say, Franny said.

But then she seemed to change her mind and quickly went into the other room. Jane waited again, but this time without noise. I sat on the couch. I thought Franny would come back into the living room and say: *You aren't allowed to see your new friend, Mattie Winokur, again.* But maybe Franny realized that would have knit a cord between us, connecting us at the breastbone. Later I understood how much she had taken on with Jane and Nan. Raising them in the summers, shaping conduct, advising where they often wanted no advice: blouses made more sense if they were tucked in; hair should be kept trim and easy to wash; smart women had careers. She insisted the girls watch *Adam's Rib* when it aired on TV. She hired the nannies who saw the girls through the winters with their messed-up mother, and she kept the family financially solvent.

It seemed a long time before she returned, and I believe she had repinned her hair. I began to poke around the living room, smelled the cigarettes in the cigarette box, tried to pick up small objects only to discover they were fastened into place.

Franny held Jane's face, kissed her cheek and whispered something that seemed to release Jane from the dining room table.

Franny focused her energies. She said something about us simply moving ahead. I was not to worry about things, which I took to mean the damage to the house.

sixteen

Standing in the doorway of the attic one evening, I hoped to be useful. I found a case of spare lightbulbs, a dozen horrible paintings from Franny's artist phase, a collection of wigs and falls. An easy chair that had lost its give. Boxes. Fans. Stuff. I thought of driving a backhoe up the stairs, scooping the contents out the attic window, or maybe using one of those refuse tubes so items could whisk down to the beach like hellions down a slide. I could bury the bulbs at sea. Maybe the hairpieces would float to Catalina. Maybe Christo would attend.

I opened a box of Christmas ornaments. The glazes on the glass were shrunken and cracked. They had gone up on the tree every year.

Mike joined me, just in from the beach. He took an ornament from my hand. Disneyland, 1975. Mickey and Goofy.

—They've been begging to go, he said.

—I'd go.

I told him about the time I went with Jane when I was twelve. How heavily it rained. The yellow plastic ponchos with Mickey on the front. Running back to the hotel periodically to put our shoes on the heaters and dry them out a little. You got the whole place to yourself that way. No waiting in lines.

Mike and I stood there eye-locked, frustrated.

—We've been so good, he said.

—So good.

—In the house anyway.

—We have been good in the house.

I pulled him in close and said:

—It shouldn't make us so miserable, being this happy.

He eased my head against his chest.

—Livvy and I talked about staying in Boston this summer.

—I almost didn't come out.

—I feel like the husband of a POW.

For a dumb, split second we kissed, which seemed to fuel the bottom door to the attic. We pulled apart as Mona's feet came up the steps.

—Who wants to play Twister? she asked, shaking the cardboard box with the happy kids on it.

I said I wouldn't mind, for a few minutes anyway, if Mike spun the dial. But as I stepped toward Mona, my foot snagged on a cord and I lost my balance. I broke my fall with my left hand, which went sailing into the open box of ornaments. Mike got me over to the window facing the beach and took the big pieces of glass out while Mona stood in the doorway. He sent her off for a tweezers, Mercurochrome, bandages, anything. But Mona seemed ill prepared. Lost.

—Just find Livvy, dear, I said.

She started down the stairs as if there were a fire that would stay on hold until someone located a hose in a vague, unspecified place and had a chance to slowly uncoil it.

—Go, Kitten, Mike said.

Mona hurried then. They wanted to take me to the hospital but I insisted on calling a cab.

The next morning Mona taught me that breakfast cereals aren't about nurturing or fueling the day. They're a delivery system providing the drug of moveable and plastic toys. Writhing, shooting, giggling things that work their way over surfaces.

—I can't get it out, she complained, her hand diving into the box, neon-colored food slipping out the top, onto table and floor. There was a jump rope tied around her ankles.

Livvy looked at my bandaged hand.

—I'll get a salad bowl, Livvy said, and stopped pouring the thread of milk on her cereal. She had been working a crossword. Livvy handed me a bowl grimy from disuse, and I washed and dried it as if I were being timed to see how fast I could do this with one hand. When I set the bowl down in front of Mona, she dumped the box's contents into it and retrieved an unidentified object wrapped in thick Mylar. Livvy put her pen down and felt the inner lip of the salad bowl.

She was kind enough not to tell me it was still damp, that we'd probably have to throw it all out.

Mona whined and tugged on the bag. I took the prize from her and quickly went into that state of madness where impenetrable synthetics shuttle me. It's easy to feel that the world is covered in plastic and you can't get in.

Livvy handed me a scissors and I snipped the bag open. A yellow toy dropped onto the table. It was round like a ball but had ears sticking out on both sides, a face painted on the front and a round knob at the bottom.

—What does it do? Mona asked.

Together we examined its moronic features.

—There have to be instructions, I said, and dredged the salad bowl with my fingers.

Livvy left her crossword again and plucked the little nut from my hands. She cleared a path on the table and ran the bottom knob rapidly over the wood, etching fine rubber lines into the surface. When she let it go, it spun to the pace of thought.

Mona watched the top.

—When's Mom coming back? she asked, squinting as if I had suddenly gone out of focus.

—She's working very hard, I know. And she misses you so much. Let's ask your dad.

I looked at Livvy. She bit her lower lip as if she was struggling for a word. When she looked at me, I thought she understood I was yielding all matters to her.

—Because Dad knows everything, she said.

I lightly touched Mona's head and then tried to work on the grocery list. Ice cream, Oreo cookies, Spanish peanuts, Coca-Cola. And I was running out of toothpaste. Here I paused. Should I buy a large tube, or would a travel-size suffice? Mona unwound the jump rope and let it drop to the floor. She was over at the freezer now, her body halfway inside, searching.

I watched her fuzzy slippers as she scraped across the kitchen, her bunchy hair momentarily pushed back in the breeze from the open French doors. When Mona surfaced with a Fudgesicle, Livvy helped her take the wrapper off. I sent them off to watch TV so I could pick up in the kitchen.

Melancholy fills from the bottom up. It's a mechanism I recognize. But devices like coffee machines that trickle down, their simple workings stymie me. I lined up the parts of the coffee maker along the counter. During my search for instructions, my elbow knocked into the glass pot and it took off into the air. I watched it smash on the black-and-white linoleum.

Counting the vases and the ornaments, this was the third breakage. I was aware that in fairy tales, rotten events come in threes.

Livvy came back into the kitchen and offered to get the broom. She handed me the dustpan. I picked out the bigger chunks of glass and dropped them in the trash, then lined up the pan for her.

—She's okay, Livvy said.

She was a deliberate sweeper, keen on getting as much glass as she could the first time through. I inched the pan around to accommodate her. I realized that whenever she and I did something together—a task like drying the dishes or grocery shopping—there was a kind of syncopation to it.

—I keep telling her she'll be back soon, Livvy said.

She stopped sweeping.

Neither of us knew what to do after that. I left Mona to choose her own cartoons upstairs but ran up a few times to see if she was hungry, if she was thirsty, if she was coming loose from her mother and needed to see me perform my stupid repertoire of sailor's knots.

seventeen

Over the next few days, I thought about splitting as a way of life. Split minds, split fields, split homes. Jane splitting. My childhood home had a solid factor of two parents but was split as if the boundaries had been set by theodolite. Split atoms.

It was my tenth birthday when Albert said I could be a radio repairman someday. No one said *radio repairwoman* then. We were spending our third summer at the rental on Miramar Beach. The boat had been dry-docked, which meant my parents were in a particularly bad mood.

—Mattie wants to play mini-golf for her birthday, Lois called across the living room, in that way we did, to be heard above the ocean noise.

Albert ignored her, lodging his head inside the back of the vintage Zenith cabinet. He had his solder gun in hand.

—But it's Wet Wednesday. So you'll take her soon. Right? she asked.

Wet Wednesday meant the sailboats raced by the sound of cannon shot off the railing of the yacht club, and Bloody Marys would be in force.

When he didn't answer, Lois picked up a credit-card bill from the table and beat it back and forth against one of her wrists. She had good hard wrists so she kept it up for a while.

I watched Albert slowly pull himself out of the body of the radio. I had taken a field trip to a zoo once and had seen a koala bear give birth. Albert's head looked the way the baby had as it emerged from its mother. I didn't tell him his hair was draped in cobwebs. Lois didn't either. He lifted his goggles and they sank into his broad, doughy forehead.

—I think we can all go today . . . since it's Mattie's birthday, he said.

Lois lit a Pall Mall, shoved the rest of the pack into a pocket in her capri pants. She wore a baggy striped t-shirt with varnish stains from working on the boat, and her sunglasses hung from a soft fraying cord around her neck.

—We aren't racing, so . . . I think we could afford to miss it once, he said.

—Can't you just see me on a mini-golf course? she asked.

I hoped my voice would skim gently over my mother's concerns.

—I don't have to go miniature golfing.

I sat on the carpet by the coffee table, which doubled as a large TV tray and depository for the kind of mail we could neither open nor toss. The remains of the previous night's Italian sat in cartons, the scent of olives and marinara and Alfredo going bad.

I tried to concentrate on my new workbook. Each time my family moved, and we did that plenty, Lois bought workbooks to make sure I wouldn't disgrace my family by falling behind. The correct age level was circled on the cover, but I think she often missed those symbols.

—Maybe you'd like to spend the day with that girl, what's her name? Lois asked.

—Jane, I said.

—You two do something fun together. It's a perfect day, she said.

And it was. Wind up, no sign of rain. Visibility strong, you could almost see the sheep on the islands. Nothing to complain about. I looked at my mother's face, tanned, unadorned, puckish. Lois liked to win her races and had plenty of placards and engraved bowls to show for it. She was the true sailor, the boat in her name. I watched her dig around in her pockets but she couldn't find anything larger than a five-dollar bill, which she began to wave in the air.

—Albert, she said.

He got out his wallet and fished out several bills, all too large. He began to fold one of them into a tiny jet.

—Would you like to do that, Pumpkin? he asked, adjusting the loft on the wings before sending it my way.

—We'll put on our thinking caps about dinner, Albert said. And a cake. We should order . . .

Lois interrupted to say:

—We have plans with that couple for after the races. Tomorrow night. We'll take Mattie for Chinese.

I felt my lower lip begin to move.

Lois's lower lip seemed to mirror mine. I don't think she realized what she was doing at first. Then she began to focus and gave Albert a leather-bound look, and said:

—I guess I should have had her in the winter months.

—You're confusing her, Albert said, and snapped his goggles back into place.

—I'm just saying a lot of races happen in the summer.

Lois screwed her eyes into a local travel guide and began to read aloud to us about fault lines.

She held up a map. Lines everywhere, like a cracked glaze.

—Imagine, she said.

—I'd like to imagine one of us unpacking, Albert said.

I looked around at the boxes, most of which remained unopened wherever we went. They were like shiftless relatives with no other shelter than the floor space we provided. My mother didn't believe in storage; she liked having her possessions close at hand, always at the ready. When she didn't answer, Albert turned to me.

—Come help me with this solder.

I started to get up. Lois looked at my unsolved geometry problems. She arched an eyebrow, and I sank back onto the rug.

—As soon as she's finished this page, Lois replied.

—She's helping me with a solder, Albert said.

—This is about her education.

Sometimes their fights would build over a number of days, their words meant to dig in slowly. Nothing we couldn't handle. But Albert looked like a raccoon prepared to fight for a trash can.

—Education? Albert said.

—I think I pronounced the word correctly.

—Good. Let's start with noise! he shouted. Your mother's pretty good at noise. Let's see.

—That's not necessary, Lois snapped. She threw the guidebook onto the table. I looked at the leftover chicken entree. The gelatinous sauce at the bottom trembled.

—There's the low-frequency hum. And that would be . . .? he asked.

—You're the only one interested in shortwaves, she said.

—About two octaves below middle C? I asked.

I quaked at the look this drew from Lois and I watched her go over to the porch doors and throw them open.

—For all to hear, she said.

Albert stood to his full height now. He wasn't a tall man, but he was burly, had a pugilist's nose.

—Then there's the hiss, he continued. And that would be . . .?

I began to shiver in my sleeveless top as the ocean air hurried into the house.

—High frequency? I asked.

—Good, Mattie. And the whistle, which is . . .?

—A high-frequency note produced, um . . .

—By unintentional audio frequency . . ., he encouraged.

—She doesn't know what the hell you're talking about.

—*Oscillations!* I called out, as if I had just won at Bingo.

—And which one is most like your mother's voice? The hum, the whistle, or the hiss?

Lois moved me aside and grabbed the container of Alfredo sauce.

I watched it arc across the room like a contrail. Albert dodged the carton and it hit the fine mesh of the radio's speakers. It flipped onto the porch, sauce rained everywhere.

—It's her fucking birthday, Albert said.

Lois went over to the bar, poured herself a gin.

I knew the stray dogs would show soon, so I closed a door to the porch when I left and ran down the beach. I saw Jane eating lunch on Franny's lower deck. She began to call to me. I hurried past the houses and the three beachside buildings of the Miramar. I scrambled below the span of the long hotel porch into the cold sand. Overhead, I could hear vacationers walking across the wood planks in flip-flops and clogs, in and out of ocean-view rooms, on their way to the snack bar, the tennis courts. The outdoor shower ran, washing off feet.

The rest happened in altered time. I think of a reel of film gradually unwinding when it's lifted out of its canister and placed flat on a table. First Jane appeared, trying to get me to talk, to come back to Franny's. A few people had gathered by then; a couple of them bent down below the lip of the porch to look at the troll, their own kids squatting close. Then I heard Franny's voice telling them everything was fine, they could go about their business. When a boy wanted to linger with his dripping Popsicle, she shooed him away.

To reach me, she had to inch through the sand on her

hands and knees in her lemon-colored silk dress, tailor-made for her in Hong Kong. It came with a matching bolero jacket but she wasn't wearing that. Her arms were bare and pale. She pressed my head against her chest so that my mucus and tears stained the silk. Jane knelt next to us and watched. Franny told her to go back to the house and see after Nan.

—We'll be there soon, she said.

Jane obeyed reluctantly. She poked along, turning back to look, as if I'd done something to her.

—I believe I cried on my . . . twelfth, or was it my thirteenth birthday? I was worried about growing old, Franny said.

She cupped a hand around one of her ears as if she couldn't hear me over the surf, but I hadn't said anything. She pulled a Kleenex out of a pocket, assured me it was clean and told me to blow my nose.

—This is the first time I've ever been under here. I guess your parents haven't been under here either, she said.

When I couldn't avoid the subject, I tried to make Lois and Albert greater than the sum of their parts. I'd boast they were members of the yacht club, as if this meant something. I think Franny saw this.

—You know about Jane's father, she said, her voice vibrating against my side.

I worried that she would go into the details. I no longer believed that his head had flown from his body. But his death was irrefutable.

—What you probably don't understand, and I'm telling

you this in confidence . . . I can do that, can't I, Mattie? Tell you something that you're never to repeat, especially not to Jane?

—Yes, I said solemnly.

—Jane and Nan's mother hasn't recovered from losing her husband. She isn't capable of . . . it's hard to explain. But that's why the girls have to put up with me in the summer.

I smelled the high note of perfume above the ocean smells, felt Franny's physical warmth. I wasn't sure what she was saying to me. I looked at the knot of bone at her wrist. She was younger than a normal grandmother, and maybe a little undernourished.

—When the girls are home they have a full-time nanny. She sees that the girls are well fed, that they get to the bus on time, that they do their homework and have nice clothes, keep up their attendance at ballet . . .

She began to show real strain now.

—When you're here in the summer, I want you to feel like you're one of my girls, Franny said.

I was aware that I should make some gesture.

—Would you teach me about furniture?

She looked at me as if I'd asked her to solve a geometry problem but I think it pleased her, once she had turned the idea over in her mind. I wasn't like Jane, who grew up with art and responded with confidence to the things she saw. She never hesitated to laugh aloud at bad stuff, no matter who the artist. But even after I had majored in art history and worked at three fairly successful auction houses, I still worried I'd be found out a fraud.

That day, after Franny coaxed me back to her house, she suggested we go for a ride. Nan was left with the neighbors for a couple of hours. Franny drove the Jaguar, and Jane and I tucked our hair into her borrowed scarves. The silk whipped our cheeks and necks as we rode and Jane and I shouted at each other in the backseat to be heard above the air currents. We watched Kleenex fly out of our purses, paper receipts, anything we could launch. Then Franny stretched her arm along the rim of the front seat, this was to let us know she wanted us to stop, her bracelets jangling. I always locked on to Franny in those moments. I saw her lavender lipstick in the rearview. The tailored suit, the way she punched in the lighter and yanked it out to meet her Camel, sparks ascending. She turned on the radio to her jazz station. She looked back at us, said we'd be amazing women. Jane pinched my arm to get me back about something and said:

—*Pay attention.*

eighteen

I put the boogie boards away in the garage and looked at the missing Jaguar. I removed a bottle of weed killer from the shelf, realizing Franny didn't have any soil, or pots or plants, other than the hibiscus. But I thought of that as being something wild. It needed little. Mostly I think she gave up on order once she left the interior of the house.

In the living room, I found Mona with her t-shirt inside out, the Velcro on her shoes ripped open. I looked at the unexpressed as she moved within inches of my face and began a staring contest. I returned a carpenter's-level gaze. Mike stopped loading his pockets.

—No one can beat Mona, Livvy said.

This cracked my solid face, and the victor handed me a brush so I could make braids out of her tangled hair.

—There's this giant whale, *ow,* and water shoots right out of its blowhole, and there's cotton candy and ducks in the pond so we're bringing bread and there's a really cool place for hide and seek. We're taking peanut-butter-and-Fluff sandwiches, and buying lemonade there. We're meeting my friends, Sienna and Charis. And Mattie, you won't get bored, *ow*.

—Chase Palm Park, Mike explained.

I noticed he had shaved.

—We could play Frisbee, Mike told Livvy.

—I have a new book.

She sat on the couch, worked on her toenails. Nudged Trader away.

—Maybe Mom's going to meet us, Mona said.

—Mom's still away, dear.

Mona turned and looked at me.

—I'd love to come but I have to go through Franny's library today.

I put the last hair band in.

Mona covered her face and Mike pumped a cloud of sunblock on her chest.

I would sort the books into piles: some for Nan, some for Jane, some for the rare-book distributor, and the leftovers into the back of the car for the used bookstore and the shelter. A few of the art books put me off but I'd take a crack. This left the ones on furniture and decorative arts. I planned to hold those out for a while.

Livvy would drift but not too far, she said.

Maybe it was night ten. I woke late in the evening to find Franny's room littered with shopping bags. I had only planned to take a nap while Mike drove the sitter home and ran to the store. The girls had gone on separate overnights.

He sat on the bed, his hand on my hip. Something was wrong. He said he had gone lingerie shopping with Dustin Hoffman, who was with his wife and daughter, browsing the Calvin Klein racks at Nordstrom's.

—Did you say anything to him?

—I looked at his wife's legs. I searched the half slips.

—You'd think he'd find a quiet boutique. You didn't see Dustin Hoffman.

—He bought things and I bought things to watch him buy things.

Mike pulled a handful of bras and undies out of a bag and let them drop back into the white tissue.

—Hope something fits.

—I don't need this much lingerie, I laughed.

—He leaned in to his wife and whispered to her . . . I couldn't make out the words exactly but his voice rolled from one end of the room to the other.

—You think they have something larger than life going?

—Oh, yeah.

—You've been crying.

—I came unglued in Nordstrom's. A clerk had to guide me to a chair outside the dressing area. She pulled the strings of the shopping bags from my fingers, someone brought me a cup of water, then another by mistake.

Jane had told me that Mike sometimes teared up at movies, but I had never believed her.

Now the concierge arrived on the escalator in her large heels and summer suit. She sat with him and looked at the satin and lace pinned to hangers in his lap. She asked if there was someone she could call.

—I would have come, I said.

—I told her about you. She told me she fell for another guy before she split with her husband.

—I'm not sure I want to know.

—It doesn't matter.

I picked up a bottle of perfume. Pulled out the applicator. I was surprised it hadn't turned to alcohol. I knew Jane had met a guy a couple of years ago. He worked as a box boy in an East Coast chain of grocery stores. Labret, hair dyed in primary colors, maybe twenty-four. It lasted a few months and then she broke it off. I didn't know if Mike knew.

—You're going to regret me. Both of you will. *Remember the time we lost a lug nut in Minnesota? Remember the time you had that thing with Mattie . . .*

—Minnesota?

I think I got my high-functioning sense of loss from Franny. The kind that often fits into the pocket of a nice suit. Something you can outline with the pencils in your briefcase. I looked at all that lingerie. When Mike attempted to hold me, the camera in his breast pocket pressed into my chest. It had been a birthday present from Jane. The size of a lipstick case. I put it on the bedside table and went off to the bathroom and took one of the tiny white biological weapons I had grown dependent on. You can't get a full night's sleep out of one and they take a while, first the fuzz state, but when they hit, you don't want to be walking around with a glass of milk or it will fly from your hands and your knees will buckle and you'll be out. Down in the spilt milk for hours. I turned on the miniature TV on the bathroom counter. CNN came on. The U.S. had started another war.

I went back to the bed and stood there, waiting for the cool blackout that quiets the bombs.

—What if Jane and I split up?

—You're asking me a what-if question.

—I'd scare you off.

—Are you splitting up with Jane?

—I don't know.

I wasn't sure which Mike he was. He wasn't the one I summoned when I paced my apartment and found no comfort in my sheets or books or food. Not the transformer that converted into different bodies, acquired different habits. He was the one I had circled for twenty years, trying to avoid. He smelled of the beach and gin and suisa and I pictured him, nestled between my legs, thirsty, afraid to dry up. And I knew if we slept together again, and he called her name, I'd probably answer.

My therapist had said many times, if my mind went too far out, I should bring it back with something immediate.

—I was thinking of making a cake tomorrow, I said. With Mona. Maybe if I describe the sauce to you. The sauce on the cake I'm thinking of making tomorrow.

I believe he said something about the past then, but I

wasn't sure what. I recall anticipating that he would pro-
duce another camera, move my arms around, tilt my head
and lower it. Almost contain me. In the marks of his lens.
If I took him in my mouth, he might turn the camera
downward and continue to shoot. But he couldn't know
everything I was thinking and he left the camera on the
night table.

I unbuttoned the top button of his shirt, as if it needed
to be freed. He pulled my khaki shorts around my ankles.
For a split second I looked over at the wares: the bustiere,
the thinly sliced thongs, the bras designed to change breasts
into endless colorful shapes. And then I let that picture go,
and sought his bitter milk.

nineteen

The thing about them, if you had seen Mike and Jane fifteen years ago walking through the Boston Common, her hand down one of his jean pockets, her laughter like a lemon peel turning in a drink, they looked like people destined for magazine culture, not wreckage.

High-gloss thinking circled their personalities. Guys on campus tracked Jane with their looks as if she was something to seek out and capture on a video screen. There was the shrimp-faced girl in my art class—flushed pink, tiny eyes, dry skin—who leaned into my ear and said she thought of Mike Waylan when she masturbated, adding:

—*I guess everyone does.*

It was easy to imagine them ducking from cameras, hurrying off in cabs, attempting to hide from the image they produced. Jane would stop and pull at her eyelashes. Mike would watch her studying the mascara on her fingers as if he believed there was something behind everything she did. People expected things of them.

Maybe this made them the perfect couple. Like JFK Jr.

and Carolyn—identities you could slip into and possess. Of course the people who wanted to inhabit them called them stupid when the plane went down. They said Carolyn was responsible. It was a circulation problem mainly: no one was supposed to take him out of circulation. She was too handsome to like, too self-confident to bury. While the Coast Guard spent millions sweeping the ocean for bits of their marriage, the media played with their rubbery mythology. But I wept openly when the news hit the air.

The first time Jane sighted Mike, we were in the school library. He was slouched in an easy chair, absorbed in a Mamet play, I think. Maybe Sam Shepard. She pointed him out with the tines of her fork and I quickly pushed her hand down so we wouldn't get caught. She had this thing about sneaking food into the library, eating under signs that read: *No food, no beverages*. I never saw a sign that said: *No sex*. But I imagine it happened, that people slipped into bathroom stalls, hid behind the giant globe.

—Look at that guy, she said.

There was a glint of anchovy paste on her lettuce.

—Did they give you a dinner roll? I asked, and opened her takeout bag, hoping for something she wasn't going to eat.

—You think he's cute, don't you?

She didn't wait for my answer. She put her salad fork down and called her friend in the Registrar's office. Jane learned that Mike was in the theater department, and switched her major from architecture to set design that afternoon.

She rarely drove her car then but Franny paid to have it parked near the college. Later that day Jane asked if I'd drive her over to this shop with bleached-out mannequins in outsized wigs in the windows. There a saleswoman learned her name, her dimensions, her desire to buy out the summer supply of lingerie. The store was close with racks and you had to step aside frequently in order to let someone go past. It was easy to get snagged on padded bra hangers. I was doing that dance when I heard the saleswoman ask Jane if her boyfriend had any particular preferences.

I watched the eager clerk push back a cuticle with one of her long, square fingernails. I wanted to say: *She hasn't even met the guy.* Jane pointed to something transparent. But mostly she gravitated toward black, as if she were dressing for a funeral. I thought about telling her I had met Mike, the day before in the cafeteria, but I didn't.

Typically, I grabbed my lunch when it was so quiet you could hear the conveyor belt looking for dirty dishes. Mike often went at the same time. He ate grilled cheese sandwiches and white cake with frosting, loaded up on small cartons of milk. Just two days earlier, he had taken a seat at my table without asking.

I had stirred my iced tea. He'd watched until I stopped.

—What do you think about before you fall asleep at night?

I had laughed and said:

—I don't know.

He introduced himself and asked me again.

—Why?

—I get this trapped feeling, he said.

He looked a little drugged around the eyes.

—I feel trapped sometimes.

He nodded, took the cellophane off his cake.

—I read the horoscopes to see if the predictions are right. You know, at the end of the day.

—Are they? he asked.

—Sometimes, I admitted. Sometimes they're right.

Mike ate the frosting, left the cake. He offered it to me and I dropped forkfuls into my mouth. My tongue moved around a known taste. He was one of those people: familiar right away. I felt as if I were driving where I could safely shut my eyes, the road curving around us. We covered a few topics.

I think he reached out for my hand then, but stopped short. Looked like he was trying not to smile. Then he got up and said:

—Maybe we could talk again?

He put my dorm phone number in his journal, next to lots of words and what looked like dried blood drops and a picture of Stephen Crane held in place with a lot of Magic Tape. Who knows? We were all a little dramatic then. I almost said: *I keep a journal.*

Instead I watched him walk around the tables and place his tray on the belt and look back at me. Things I didn't say made smooth tracks through my brain—little snails of thought.

I dropped Jane off at her dorm, parked the car, and went back to my place. That night I played the cafeteria scene over as if I were trying to pick lyrics off an album. I should have taken his number down in my notebook. I was lying in bed next to a naked boy named Stuart while I thumbed through a magazine. Stuart liked to tell me scary things about the human body before he fell asleep. I think it was his effort to understand his identification with premeds. He would push his head between my legs or into an armpit, rooting, trying to get somewhere.

I found my horoscope and read it aloud to him.

—Love is imminent but might be a problem. You can keep it from being a problem if you keep an open mind, but you should avoid triangles.

—Ever take chemistry? he asked.

I wondered how Stuart breathed, wedged into me like that.

—I know a triangle is a stable shape, I said.

—Difficult to break apart, he added, lifting himself and staring into my navel.

Avoid triangles, I wrote in my journal. *Avoid love.*

When Jane introduced us, Mike and I pretended we were meeting for the first time. We didn't coordinate it that way, it just happened. If she saw something awkward there, she didn't say.

Sometimes I went to rehearsals and watched, sitting in the back row, my chin against the red velvet seat in front of me. Mike was on lighting. He came up and disappeared in colored gels. Jane was crew. I told her she should act. She had the face, the poise unless you understood the nervous understructure, which I don't think most people saw. She memorized lines quickly, sometimes giving prompts. It's possible she couldn't take direction, but when she hit the stage to bring out a prop, the lighting guys, the cast, they looked. And when Mike and she were up on stage together, my mind seesawed between them.

I watched, I did my homework, I had out-of-body experiences that I didn't tell anyone about because I know they had to do with looking at Mike under the lights. Auras, maybe. It's possible we have them.

We talked a little, mostly when Jane was busy.

After they began to see each other regularly, she spent a lot of time over at Mike's. His mattress was on the floor, sometimes Jane washed his sheets. He lived in a neighborhood where junkies hung out, though he had money to get a decent place. She told me they did erotic stuff, often by the open window of Mike's bedroom, where she kept hundreds of dollars' worth of lingerie stuffed in his closet. He never bothered to buy a dresser. I wasn't sure I needed to hear all the secrets.

I know it was his taking off that drained her. He used to be the one to vanish. He would throw his shoes and jacket into his smoothly Bondoed Thunderbird, the salmon-colored filler along one side, rimming a headlight, and down the center of the hood to hide the dents. Sometimes Mike left her a note, but it wouldn't say much. And when he came back from wherever he'd been he'd have a Mardi Gras mask, a gravestone in the backseat of his car, a bruised face, stories about his whereabouts that didn't make sense. He made his first film in a cemetery, skipped a lot of classes. I don't think Jane realized he was shooting up speed. I imagined he'd outgrow it and that she'd outgrow him. Then they talked about getting married.

He eased up on the hard drugs when a friend of his went blind on the stuff, and eventually quit altogether. I think he learned how to store his uncapped energy in the calm of running imagery, the ability to splice and rejoin film. The big shift appeared to happen after Livvy was born. But I was never sure if Jane fully appreciated this change. I think she still wanted him walking edges of high buildings. But not really. Not at all. He had made her life safe, she needed safety, craved it as anyone would.

There was one weekend when Jane was down in New York and Mike dropped by my apartment unannounced. We lived pretty close to each other at the time, in Somerville. He used the tiny door knocker. I looked through the equally small window in the door. He asked to come in.

Seeing his face screwed me up. When I did let him in he made me sit on the lumpy couch with him. Pigeons flew up from the parking lot and swung by my living room windows, two or three of them stood on my sill. We both sat without movement and watched. I don't know about pigeons, some people believe they're just dirty. But I think that's simple.

I straightened my clothes or lit some matches or moved

the coasters around. Most of the audio on this one is missing. Maybe we discussed books or movies. He was at that stage when he resisted his father's trade. His father was a film editor. It's possible Mike wanted to push it away because he'd discovered he was good at it.

It broke my heart, sitting there like that. The sense that we should have been together. This was the place where the cloth was marked with chalk to say: *Here. Right now. Alter things from this point down, the sleeves, everything, or live with the way things fit.* It's not that he wasn't good for Jane, but it didn't help that I felt like we were in a scene from *Roman Holiday* when he kissed me. Mike would have stayed the night if I'd let him. I should have. I almost did. But it wasn't like I could blot Jane out. And she was always going through something, with her mom and all. So I told him I had . . . what was it? . . . a canker sore, a date, a loose hip?

I decided it was better to wait until she had tired of him. Jane had never stuck with any guy for more than three months. I offered him something to eat before he took off. I made him eggs with thawed spinach and Uncle Ben's converted rice.

Years later, after I had moved to Chicago, I ran into that boy Stuart. He lived in an apartment on the far North Side, and he convinced me to come over for a drink. My therapist had been on this jag about my taking more risks. It was sort of like Aesop's fables. As if the point of therapy is to outwit a variety of beasts, only to find them all sitting outside the door again, begging to come in.

I agreed to stop by one night after work. Stuart had a job painting over graffiti, and had just come home. He offered me a beer that he squeezed out of his mini-fridge. His hair and his neck and the backs of his hands were spattered with paint. We watched the elevated trains go by. I thought about risk when he slid toward me on his couchbed. I had my diaphragm in my purse, condoms.

He said the bathroom was through the curtains and off to the right. I went into a bolt of loosely hung velvet filling a door frame, and suddenly dropped down a step. The room was dark except for the flickering light at the end of a hall. I couldn't find a switch so I went for the light. When I pushed a door back, I found a naked couple on a mattress on the floor, fucking.

If I had to give an accident report, I would say she had her ankles braced against his shoulders and he had long blond hair gathered into a ponytail. I didn't stay to watch, but enough skidded through my mind, and I was struck by how mechanical and meaningless their act looked.

I went back through the curtain, trying to think of a way to explain my sadness to Stuart. He was pretty well stoned by then. Before I could come up with anything, he said:

—*I was sick with love for you that way.*

twenty

Mona and Mike were thickly settled upstairs. Livvy was off in Catalina with Taylor's family. I had moved through a few hours of Ambien when I heard the radio going. I got up from the couch and inched down the hall in the pitch dark. When I stepped into the kitchen, the bright green numbers of the digital clock blinded me: three A.M. I clicked off the news update, feeling like I was having one of those things. Between sleeping and waking. A state. I was having a state. I opened the fridge and clung to the door, looking at the eggs and whipped cream, the takeout boxes and uneaten cold cuts. I was hungry but full.

I jumped when I heard something drop to the floor, maybe a spoon. There was Jane, standing in the dark corner of the kitchen with some guy. She was pressed against him, his arm locked around her waist.

I turned away, counted, breathed, looked at the cool air swirling out of the fridge, around the Coca-Cola bottles, through the hole in my chest. I clicked on the light over the stove and faced her.

—This is Neal, she said, still in his grip.

Neal was: uneven blue plaits, huge plugs in each ear-lobe, I guessed twenty-two, I imagined Burger King once a week for the toy, an authenticity to every bungee dive he took, a boy who knew how to wake up before he hit the ground. He must have had a whole world of mappage going on underneath his pants and t-shirt: tattoos, piercings, the works.

—This is Neal? I asked, as if I'd gotten bad directions and found myself driving through the wrong town.

I don't think she had a plan in mind, a next step. I couldn't believe how thin she had become. She was wasting away in a flowered rayon dress, the kind you can pull off the rack at T. J. Ben for $15.00. Her eyes puffy. But I think we all looked tired.

—What the fuck are you doing? I asked.

I could almost make out the heat as it moved off her skin, through the air like a vapor trail. She took a seat at the table. When she opened her mouth to answer, Neal said:

—I've got to have some coffee.

—Your boy here has to have some coffee, I said.

Neal looked at me like I was a puzzle he could do, no problem. Jane reached for his hand and he took the seat next to her. She had blue dye on her fingertips. I pictured them having met on the deck of Nepenthe at Big Sur or at a gas station among the giant sequoias. This guy wasn't as big as Bunyan but he had plenty of lean muscle mass. Maybe they both liked the same kind of pie and had found each other at a restaurant counter. Then I realized who it was. She had circled back to something familiar, or had never unplugged from it.

—You need a sleeping bag, Neal? Because Mike's in the big bed and you might find things a little crowded up there, I said.

Neal chuckled. He appeared to be unwaiting, open to cues.

—He's just dropping me off on his way to LA.

Neal whispered something to Jane while putting a sympathetic hand on her back. Her look was weary then vibrant. Like a hologram, the picture changed and then changed back. I didn't understand how it worked, how things flattened and then suddenly took on dimension with her. I watched her thumb slide back and forth over the webbed place between Neal's thumb and forefinger.

Jane laughed. When she saw the coffee bag, she said:

—Who likes *Kenyan?*

Now she had me amused.

—You know, the store was out of French roast and the guy who stocks the specialty coffees? He was right there on-site. He recommended Kenyan as a substitute for your favorite. Always good to have a solid substitute on hand, he said.

—Put a little milk in mine? Jane asked.

She reached down and picked up a tablespoon from the floor, wiped it off, and used it to dig into the sugar bowl.

—You keeping him? I asked.

—There's a vitality to your jealousy. Usually it's sluggish. But there, always there, she said.

I looked at the gouge in the vinyl flooring where Franny had once dropped an iron pot. Jane's toenails were painted a sloppy white. Maybe after she had finished dying Neal's hair blue and plaiting it she had put her feet up on a stack of motel pillows so he would have a clear reach at her toes. I don't imagine they had any cotton balls or polish remover, just an impulse buy—a single bottle of polish at a convenience store.

—Why are you doing this?

—You're so full of shit.

—And that means what *exactly?*

—That means Mike. He's all over your face.

—I'll get the stuff, Neal said, heading toward the back door.

—Yeah, you go get the stuff, Neal, I said.

—You're tripping, he said to me.

—Warming up for the trip, I said.

I had to get out of there. I went into the living room to start packing but Jane flew up behind me. She reached into my suitcase and threw some of my clothes around. Mostly lingerie. She gave me a look.

—This is what *you* wanted, I shouted and tried to shove things back into my suitcase again.

—Do you get that? *You*. Not me, I said.

—You've always wanted Mike.

—What are you looking for? You want the wrapping paper back? The ribbon? The Magic Tape?

—The game's off, she said.

The key latch on my suitcase appeared to be broken. I was trying to force it into place.

—Game? You're the only one who's playing, I said.

—You pulled the same shit with Franny. Pushed your way in. Do you know what she called you? Poor Mattie. She didn't say your name once without putting *poor* in front of it.

—Do you see what you're doing? Or do you just have to be an impulsive, blind fuck to hurt so many people all at once?

That was when Neal returned with a load of things for the house. For some stupid reason we stopped and watched as if he were demonstrating a product we might buy. I guess that was the way we fueled up for the next round. It was painful to see Franny's blue luggage return. I thought this was one thing we had gotten rid of. He went about his job, making neat stacks against the wall. There was a doll for Mona, a new tennis racket. For Mike? When Neal was done, he put his arms around Jane and slid his hands down her back as if he were searching for his brand. We were all surprised when Mike came through the doors to the lower deck. Maybe he had gotten up early or had never gone to sleep. I considered that he might have sat by the couch and watched me sleep and tried to make some kind of decision, finally going out for a smoke. He held an empty glass.

—You're bringing them home now? he asked. His hair stuck up in a funny way, no pajama top.

Jane pulled away from Neal, signaled for him to leave but he stood there.

—Are you the lawn-care specialist? Mike asked. Or the guy who works at the batting cages? Maybe the certified plumber. Help me out here, Jane. Which one is this?

—I race catamarans, Neal said. I was just dropping your wife off on my way to a race.

—Is that what you're doing? Because to me, it looks like you're trying to make a total asshole out of me.

Mike circled Neal. Jane started to back up.

—Our lawn doesn't need a specialist, she said.

—Go to hell, Mike said.

—And I don't like baseball and what was the third one? Is there something wrong with the plumbing? He's just a boy, Mike, and he needs to get on the road.

—Do you hear yourself? Mike asked.

—I think her hearing is great, Neal said. Everything about her is great.

I almost laughed aloud. The burlesque of it. Neal's serious intent. Jane's flight to the cigarette box. My inability to lock my suitcase.

—You know, Mike, I'd say we're pretty even here. One for you, one for me.

I watched Jane's hands shake as she lit a match.

—Mattie, leave the fucking suitcase alone! Mike shouted.

As he said this, the glass he held slipped out of his hand and he kicked it out of the way.

—This is too random, Neal said, turning to go.

Mike shoved him into the bookcase.

—Don't let . . ., I began.

In the second Mike looked away, Neal got in a swing, which landed solidly on Mike's left cheek, just below his eye. As he fell back, his foot came down on one of Mona's small wheel-driven toys. He twisted sideways as he fell, smacking his head on the sharp edge of the TV cabinet. He put his hand up to his head. I'd never seen so much blood. I ran upstairs to get towels, shouting for him to be still. Telling them to call 911.

Mona was sitting at the top of the steps. I almost ran into her.

—Go be with your mom, Kitten.

—I'm okay, Mike said. It's just a cut.

I heard the sound of a four-cylinder engine as I ran back with the towels. Neal had left and Mona clutched her mother's legs. But Jane was unavailable. She couldn't stop crying. The first beach towel soaked through. When I removed that one to apply another, I swear I saw Mike's brain. I commanded Mona to breathe. She pulled away long enough to hand the phone to me.

twenty-one

Here's one way people are expunged: They are taken up in airplanes, sedated, and pushed from open hatches. It's possible this originated in Argentina.

I was flying across the San Fernando Valley toward home. I sat in a window seat, and the large man in the middle talked to me. He distributed athletic equipment. About the time he got into Pilates balls, I swear I heard the cargo hatch open.

He said his product line was different because he was brilliant on the service end. Then he asked for my cake if I had no plans of eating it.

When my suitcase dropped from the plane, it came undone and the contents flew up and off. I believe it headed for a Frosty Freeze or a high school heating vent out on the plains.

—You see that? I said.

—What?

—The ground. Can you see the ground from your seat?

I handed the man my cake. Maybe he saw a broken energy around my head, because he reached for the flight-attendant button. But I touched his arm and he handed me my glass of water instead.

—You ever have forty stitches in your head? I asked.

—I got ten once. Football.

—Someone I know got stitches from his temple almost to his hairline, at the back of his head. But he's fine.

I couldn't find my reading glasses and gave the guy my bottle of sleeping pills and asked if he would count them and tell me if there were ten left. If there were ten, not nine, I should be good to go. I don't remember after that until I was on the ground and a flight attendant nudged me awake.

When I got home, I turned on the oscillating fans and the neon. I watched the mild power surges as I stood dumbly in front of the open spoil of the refrigerator. I walked over to the neighborhood market and when I returned I realized there was someone's *Scientific American* and a dog chew toy in my grocery bags.

While I sipped my Kenyan coffee at the counter, I thumbed through and read an article on synesthesia. It described a man who experiences a bitter taste when he touches ground meat and a woman who sees blue whenever she hears C-sharp.

I had never heard of this state. Somehow two sensory perceptions are experienced simultaneously in a brain cross-wire, one sense slightly in front of or behind the other. Some people with synesthesia see colors when they

look at letters, some hear shapes or taste music. It's not supposed to be pleasant or unpleasant but simply the way certain individuals attend life. But this was where the blue
angular morning overtook me. The authors said the study
might shed light on the reasons some people are prone to
the easy use of metaphor, all that "excess communication
among different brain maps."

I looked at the white and yellow of the fried eggs and
thought about links between the seemingly disparate. With
Jane, I wasn't sure how we cross-wired, but we always had.
I didn't understand, in our overlay, if she was slightly in
back or slightly in front of me. With Mike things had been
much more straightforward, effortless. We simply overlaid.

I wondered if I should have taken the train home as a
way to deal. A broad expanse seen from an observation car,
Kansas at night. Under that kind of bubble, I might have
been able to come to a decision about selling the loft. If I
didn't line up a job soon I'd be forced to sell. I thought
about relocation, career switching, returning to school, in-
jections, but which kind? If I could afford a slip, I might
live on a boat. My parents had talked about that periodically. I tried to imagine this toddler learning to walk while
Lois and Albert pitched about. For the first time I was glad
I had rarely gone out.

It was 95 degrees, Chicago-humid. I called the house and
was relieved when Livvy answered. She told me Mike
was fine. She described the scar again. She said they sent

him right home. We talked a little and I said I'd love it if she could come out sometime. When I hung up, I soaked a sheet in cold water and drew it over my body as I stretched out on the bed and dropped off.

The next morning, the Thunderhead Diner sign above my bed washed the room in blue. I cracked open a toaster treat and had that with coffee, walking out to the porch. From the second floor the view was: wood frame and brick, garden walls, bits of Wells and North Avenue, cars. If I went to the other end of the loft and crawled out onto the fire escape, I could see the Boys Club where they cooked teriyaki chicken once a year for the art faire.

My neighbor was out on her porch with her *Trib,* drinking a highball. She rarely spoke to me other than to express her unhappiness with my approach to garbage re-moval. Now she looked at me and said:

—You're lucky you didn't lose your gardenias.

I imagined she had come over to water them in thimblefuls—just enough to guarantee survival and show me up. I went back inside.

Under normal circumstances, I always went through a crash or at least a shift after returning from Franny's. I could never think straight after two or three weeks on that beach, going out to swim with the same small group of people in that buoyant salt water, the endless recreation. You watched the ocean and the drop as the boats fell off the flat Earth. You got bloated and full of fish and wine and you thought the world runs that way.

On my message machine, I listened to an opportunity to stay in Williamsburg at a discount, a plea for funds from my alma mater, a jokey kind of message from Clark sitting around in his black boxer shorts drinking mai tais. I heard my boss's voice at the auction house. He said the estate of a lozenge manufacturer was about to change my life.

A big name in Chicago, this guy owned a stadium, golf courses, high-rises, and land that department stores stood on. I would be in charge of the fine arts and antiques in his main house on the North Shore. Katie, who typically handled the largest properties, was getting married to one of our clients, taking a year or two off to travel. *Reorganizing her priorities,* my boss said. I'd been put in charge of a home without sentimental items to snag on. Clothing and other personal effects had already been handled by a senior member of the household staff, in conjunction with the family. There would be no meds in bathroom cabinets.

It seemed money would continue to move through uninterrupted and I would float for a while, belly down, trying not to look through the slats of the raft.

Sex with Clark worked the way a well-lubricated cruller machine does when it cranks out product unerringly. The right form, the drop into the oil, the rise to the surface. I got off, he got off. Afterward, he went into the bathroom to wash up and prepare a warm cloth with a hand towel for me. There was no mess with Clark. I listened to the courtyard sounds through the open windows.

The neighbor kids were home from school. A ten-year-old named Ginger dared another girl to jump back and forth over the lid of the incinerator. It was fastened down with an iron padlock. But sometimes I thought, if that lock broke, Ginger had the power to coax this girl to leap into the next world. I threw on my robe and yelled out the open window:

—That's not safe, Ginger.

One of the boys laughed at her.

I went into the kitchen and came back with a package of Nilla Wafers and one of Mystic Mints. I asked them to play somewhere else and sailed the cookies down between the buildings. They ate down to the broken bits and ran off. But they returned minutes later as if the sky might bring forth more cookies.

I turned away. Clark stood in the middle of my bedroom with spa supplies. He was prepared to wash and oil me, sprinkle me with dusting powder, a Turkish towel draped over his arm.

—I use that in my shoes, I said. That powder. Trying to get him to smile.

—I haven't seen you in three months.

I sat down on the bed. He placed the washcloth in my hands and tossed the other items onto the spread.

—I just don't . . . like baby powder. I . . .

Clark laughed.

—It's a good thing you've never been in love, Mattie.

It didn't seem fair to tell him. He showered and changed into the fresh set of black clothes he had rolled into his duffel. Then he went down to the neighborhood grocery, as if I had the flu and someone had to look after me. He was that way. He brought bags of food and paper towels and dryer sheets and put things away, ordered me to call him.

Livvy wrote this e-mail: *Taylor wants to hook up with me. Think he's worth it? Mom looks through just one stupid box of old junk, then starts crying and goes upstairs to lie down. Dad sleeps in the living room now. He takes Mona and me to the Coral Casino, makes a buffoon of himself, like we need that kind of humor to balance something out. I think my crawl is getting better. I guess he's going to take Mona back to Boston for a while. Write back if you want, but keep it generic. Mona misses you.*

I wrote: *livvy—generically speaking, i'm not sure i'd bother. i think it would leave you . . . blank or maybe chilly. cold energy spreads and can fill more space than you intend. if this is confusing, i'm free to make it worse over the phone.*

I know things are crazed right now and they might be that way for a while, but then they'll change. hang in. mattie

I got dressed and headed toward Lake Michigan on foot, through the commercial strip of Wells Street, past Ripley's Believe It or Not. Into Lincoln Park, I bisected the lawn of the Historical Society and went by the small tomb with the name *Couch* raised on the granite above the gate. No other graves, just the isolated mausoleum of Couch. I wondered about the Couches. If they'd all agreed to be buried in a stack in their permanent home or if there had been divisive arguments that bumped some of them out to small rural plots.

I sat for a while on a bench between the lake and the Drive. Lucky folk in their high-rise apartments, lucky views, the rush of cars. Bicyclists, runners, engagement. I let the glare off the water work on my eyes, scanning for a head-ache. I ate two hot dogs, hoping the nitrates might create cranial pressure and prompt some kind of knowing. I fun-neled in sugar: an extra-gulp Coca-Cola, ice cream bar with a bubble-gum center, blue cotton candy. But I remained transmissionless. Stuffed. Buzzing with blank energy.

It wasn't that I believed I had a chance at Jane's life, or understood this concept, or even wanted it. But I had leaned in too close, turned the dial past its reception point. I had picked up a signal, the voice had been responsive, animated, hopeful, but it had arrived from the wrong country.

The estate was a land of candy dishes with wrapped lozenges in every room. Two Maseratis in the garage. I wanted to go somewhere but I couldn't find the keys. I read up on hot-wiring. I talked to my mechanic. Eventu-ally I would take one out. I would get over my fear of bad electricity.

There were ten bathrooms, seven bedrooms, a private beach fronting the lake, a boathouse. No one to kick my shoes off the bedspreads. I found suits and towels, sarongs, and caps in the cabana, went out for long swims in the lake. I set up my laptop in one of the sitting rooms, used binoculars for distraction, chipped away at this guy's life, happy to be doing the one thing I knew well. Saw service-people come and go. The mansion had gone through end-less architectural and interior tweaking and rooms seemed to fight each other by color and design, like the warring factions of a family. But some of the ceilings were im-ported from sixteenth-century churches. I looked up and suffered heaven from overstuffed couches.

I was told his heirs wanted straight-up cash. The art-work was cacophony and nothing significant in all that noise. Some copies. All to be cataloged and sold. Months of work. I heated the sauna, sent my employer optimistic e-mails on my progress. Finger foods and a variety of fresh salads and breads arrived daily. But I raided the pantry and made peanut-butter-and-Fluff sandwiches and ate the Turbo Pies. The recesses of the kitchen were heavy in junk and it was weird and calming to be at the beach again. Maybe some point could be made about life's circularity, but then wheels would start to crowd my brain. I gave up on metaphor and ate.

Mattie—I think Taylor's seeing someone but he hangs out. He started building Franny's Snow White puzzle. You know the one with a thousand white pieces. Mom and Dad aren't speaking or have these mock conversations. He takes Mona back to Boston to-morrow. Did you ever run an auction or do you just appraise stuff?—Livvy

. . . . . .

I looked for something to happen. Not the obvious stuff: the car accident, or Lou Gehrig's disease, or apoplexy. Maybe just the cave-in of the bathroom ceiling in my loft. My upstairs neighbors' tub had overflowed several times before I'd moved in and I wasn't sure how the repairs had been handled. Now there was a bubble in the wallpaper above my tub, a large brown circle. I needed it to give way. I needed some kind of distraction so I wouldn't have to think about Mike.

The only real distraction came when I was knocked out. It seemed I was bumping into chair legs and refriger-ator handles in order to eat in my sleep. There were drops of chocolate on my sheets in the morning, an ice-cream container tipped over, spoon stuck in it, in a pool of goo on my bedside table.

The phone rang sometimes. Clicks I couldn't identify. I answered Livvy's e-mails promptly.

Mattie—Mom's spirits better but not to be trusted. Mona told her she loved her a million times this morning, as if this will keep her from going away again. Dad and Mona took a taxi to the air-port so he could take her back east to see our cousins. I wish I was old enough for a license. Mona's breaststroke really improved the last few days. In four weeks we'll be back in the school I hate. Mary the Realtor, frustrated that her calls aren't being returned, seeks me out for conversation.—Livvy

Livvy—Tell Mary you just got your real estate license and plan to handle this one alone.—Mattie.

. . . . . .

I saw friends. And Clark and I got together on a couple of occasions. Once, outside his apartment door, around two A.M., I hoped the dread of waking up his conservative neighbor or her husband, the concern that one of them would step into the hall fully robed and slippered, standing by the *No solicitors* sign on their door, might enable me to feel vivid. But the contact with Clark was airless. What had seemed organic now hinted of bad bearings.

I turned off the ringer on my phone.

I sprinted out of the shower when I realized Mike's voice was coming through the machine. Knocking the water from my ears, I grabbed the receiver just as he hung up. When I tried to retrieve the message, I got so nervous I erased it by accident. I wanted to call back.

twenty-two

She called from O'Hare and I drove out to pick her up. There were red streaks in her hair now, cuffs on her ears. New tattoos up her calves. She would admit later she had applied those on board while a woman with a laptop had looked on, as if she were something on a DVD. Livvy had crammed a few things into a leopard-skin carry-on, so there was nothing to pick up in baggage. She looked older, somewhat like Jane did in college. I couldn't quite get how she did that, but she was willing to show me her fake ID.

—You running away? I asked.

—Not running running.

I waited until we were in the parking lot to hand her my phone, and got her to call her mom. When she tried to hand it to me, insisting I had to say something, I asked her to hold the receiver near my mouth. *Livvy's always welcome!* I shouted, as if no one would ever be able to hear me. Then Livvy hung up.

. . . . . .

My room had the better neon and the good quilt. So I changed the sheets and put out magazines. I think she liked this in her mute way. I pointed out which towels were hers and nodded toward the hotel soap I had unwrapped and placed in the soap dish. She left the bathroom and crawled into the covers and was quickly knocked out. I crashed in the tight sheets of the guest room, happy to have her company.

At eleven-thirty the next morning, Livvy passed her invisible host in the hall, showered, and ate two untoasted bagels with slabs of saltless butter. She returned to her room and got back into bed.

—I'm sorry I don't have much in the fridge. There's a bakery . . . not as good as the one by Franny's but . . .

I got out a coil of incense from the bedside table and put it on a plate Livvy had used for her bagels.

—When I had sex with Taylor, right in the middle, the phone rang. He answered it.

—Oof. At his house?

—Catalina. His parents were out golfing. It's so weird that he'd fucking answer the phone.

—Do you know who called?

—I think it was this girl who likes him.

—I'm sorry.

Livvy moved over and I put my head on the pillow next to hers. I saw her move her mouth as if she were trying out words to fit the space.

—I'm no good at figuring these things out, Livvy. Do you want to see him?

—I guess. But probably not. Mom took off again. For two days. I saw this guy from the clock-room windows. It was four in the morning. He was waiting out back by his BMW. I'd seen him once before. Everybody's so screwed up.

I heard a rich hollow sound in my head. Someone was taking a shower in the apartment above. I wanted to run around the building and tell all my neighbors to turn on their taps full blast and flood the building. I wanted to be straight up with her, make my confessions. I wanted to tell her about the tectonic plates of guilt, about being in love with her dad. But that wasn't any good. She didn't need to hold my place for me.

—I'm getting Franny's books. The ones on fine arts and furniture, she said.

She didn't ask where we were going but simply dressed and followed me to the old Peugeot. She took out a notebook and clicked her retractable pen a lot. I saw my name scribbled, then crossed out, but I had to downshift and she snapped her notebook shut. We passed the high-rises on Sheridan. Then the estates along the lake appeared. The North Shore.

When we arrived at the mansion, she took several shots of the entrance with a disposable underwater camera, tracking something through the house from her heavy

boots, maybe tar. I decided to let it go. There were main-
tenance men, rug cleaners, things I could do.

She went through the living room, ran her fingers along
the keyboard of the white baby grand, and tripped out to
the pool, where she disappeared from sight. A little later I
heard the even strokes of her crawl. I watched the pool
through the binoculars. The temporary red streaks trailed
from her hair into the water, dissolving, or maybe it was
the light reflected off the berry bushes.

When she woke me from a nap, she dripped blue chlo-
rinated water onto the Persian rug.

—Here's what I think, she said.

I sat up on the couch and shaded my eyes from the late-
afternoon light.

—You could show me how to run an auction.

—Ah, an auction. There aren't any auctions this week.
But we could talk about them.

Livvy sat on a hassock and moved her mood ring
around from her thumb to her middle finger and back
again.

—You're not supposed to get them wet, she said.

—No?

—It changes your mood. Now it's stuck on dark blue.

I told her how we arrived at values and how we dis-
played things, if we put objects in groups or let them stand
alone. The order in which we brought pieces out to build
momentum, that was significant. I told her about the
agents who sit on the phones and what it's like to understand people's signals, the way you might coax a little more

out of a room with inflection, how you can play people off one another for the good of the sale, and a little bit about the personalities of the buyers.

—Sometimes it's like being in pictures of time, all run together. You know. Runner's high. Auctioneer's high. Swimmer's . . .

—You don't stress? she smiled.

—You even get high off that.

I think I'd held this illusion when Livvy had called from the airport: that she would instruct me so I could find out what primary color to dye my hair. We would take taxis to boutiques and restaurants, run over my credit cards like brainless squirrels dashing across Michigan Avenue. Hit a few galleries, take in a couple of plays. I would show Livvy off to friends. She would introduce me to swimming technique and CDs. I would get my nose pierced with a tiny stud. But after she was there for a day, I began, instead, to feed her impulse, this funny new desire to learn something about the business. I took her to the office, showed her the books and catalogs, my list of dealers, sources used in making appraisals. Then I took her through the property stored for the next auction.

Livvy and I returned to the loft that evening to find the smells of lime and onion and cilantro in the stairwell. My front door was cracked open, and Clark greeted us. I had forgotten that he and I had talked about getting together that night, pre-Livvy. He still had his key.

In the kitchen, he returned to his enchilada assembly. A black chef's apron hung from his neck. He was shirtless. Livvy gave him a studied look, went over to a pot cooling on the stove, and scooped out a spoonful of white rice.

—Livvy. Jane's daughter. Clark, I said.

He tried to make conversation, asked about her school, if she went out for sports. She did her best to answer using a precise combination of yes and no and um.

Finally I said:

—You're ignited, Clark.

There was a brief lag before he whipped around and pulled a blackened tortilla off the burner.

—We have plenty, he said. Don't worry.

—Are you guys having a date? Livvy asked.

She went over to the sink. I think she was trying to read my fortune somewhere in the dirty dishes.

—Are we having a date? he asked me.

I shook my head.

—I didn't think so, Livvy said.

I can't blame him for looking put off. He poured some tequila and a can of frozen margarita mix into the Oster-izer. Flipped on the switch. I could tell by the butcher paper that he had gone to my favorite market. Probably swordfish or tuna from California. Wild salmon. A good bottle of chardonnay. Fresh raspberries. I rested a hand on Clark's shoulder, then I reached around and pulled the plug on the blender.

Clark and I walked down the hall to the door. I apologized and tried to explain that we should probably make it another night. That I'd call him. I think I even added the word: *honest.*

I released his arm.

—Just send my shirt back . . . unlaundered.

He handed me the key.

—I shrunk the last one, didn't I?

—Yeah.

I gave him a kiss and watched him jaunt down the front stairs. He was still wearing my oven mitts when he walked outside.

twenty-three

After dinner Livvy got on the phone and I went off to the neighborhood bookstore. It started to rain, and after a while I ran under the eaves of the Laundromat to wait it out. I was umbrellaless and my sweater had soaked through. In the movies, when they do a rain scene, the crew adds a little milk to the water to make it more visible. I could see the milk when I looked down the street.

A woman sat inside with her kids. I had seen them there before. She stared at the bank of industrial dryers as if her fatigue were a dish towel going round and round. One of her boys repeatedly punched the buttons on a vending machine that dispensed detergents and plastic bags. He stood on a chair and kicked it. He wasn't putting coins in. He just wanted delivery.

There was something about her stasis, her inability to meet her son's demands, that pulled a trigger in me. I certainly didn't expect her to purchase fabric softener or make him sit quietly in a chair to satisfy my sense of abandonment. And maybe he did this all the time, pushed at candy-bar levers, inoperable cigarette machines, so it was no big deal. But I heard Franny's voice as if she were five feet away. She was humming to a jazz riff. I didn't know how this projection of sound found me in a downpour. But I felt that I'd had a visitation.

I think my father signaled me when he died two years before Franny. I had to get a storage unit in Florida close to their apartment. We had buried Lois three years earlier and my parents had twenty-five cartons of stuff I'd never seen them unpack. Sailing trophies, I imagine: they had a whole lot of those boxed and labeled. Radios. Static. A single mover helped me, a fraternity boy who went to the university in Tampa and loved his life. He had short, standup hair and waxless ears. As he loaded boxes onto his pickup, we heard a radio start up inside a carton. It felt as if my father were talking to me.

—Sounds like the Cubs are playing, the guy said. Maybe we should open her up.

—It'll wear itself down, I said.

Which prompted him to tell me something about the Cubs and the kind of wear a team can go through.

I asked him if he'd like it . . . the whole box. Take it, I said.

Maybe this resignation drove him to have a curiosity about me. Whatever it was, we fucked in a damp motel room five miles from an alligator farm. Later I wished I'd gone to see the alligators.

I paid the storage facility fee every month for years. Never went back, never had things shipped out—couldn't, though I tried to work myself up to it. The next time I went through my bills, I tossed out the one from the Safe Right Storage in Clewiston, Florida. I hoped the owners would take what they could, sell what they couldn't, forget about me.

I've always liked whole stories. Miniatures. Complete, detailed accounts. Some of them full of remorse. Lois gave me fragments. So there was nothing to unbox with her.

I went back to my loft and Livvy buzzed me in.

twenty-four

Mike sent me five letters after I left Franny's. Each one in an old envelope from the Miramar Hotel. Franny used to save that stuff, stationery, swizzle sticks. He must have grabbed them from her desk. I decided I couldn't read them at first and put them in a hat box in the closet, put the hook on the closet door to keep it from swinging open. In the morning, I'd find them on top of my bedding. I realized I must have been reading them in my sleep. I'd quickly stuff them back into their envelopes and put them away again.

The migraines rolled in but told me little. I could smell my neighbor's highballs in her dark apartment at night and the dead water that dripped out of air conditioners two blocks away. I focused on work and went out some nights with friends.

Jane called.

—I only have time to talk with Livvy, she said.

—She's in the tub.

Mona had informed me, that summer, that when a

goldfish stops, it either floats to the top of the tank or curls
and drops to the bottom.

—Tell her to pull the plug. I'll call her in ten minutes.

I did, and heard the water going on and off intermit-
tently to draw any last bits of hot water out of the pipes.
When Livvy produced herself, I saw the half-dozen candles still burning around the tub. Steam on the mirror, the
moist buckled wallpaper. She didn't like to break up the atmosphere with the overhead fan.

Livvy threw herself on my bed, the portable phone in
her wet hand. She pushed the bedroom door shut with her
foot. Then she was up and staring into the freezer while
Jane, I assumed, waited on the other end again. She took a
pint of premium ice cream back to my room, the door
closed, the conversation reentered.

I heard her yell, then she turned up the volume on the
radio and yelled some more.

I saw the color of her bathrobe as she flew back and
forth from bedroom to bathroom, applying makeup, the
phone gone now.

That night Livvy was up when I went to sleep, coma-
tose in the morning, pushed ahead with whatever she was
doing. She'd drawn streaks of red and white from her eyebrow to her cheekbone, and the colors had smeared on my
pillowcases. I think she'd copied this look out of one of my
*Vogue*s. I think she wanted to hide—as I did.

Most days we drove out to Lozenge World. We left
peeled candy wrappers on countertops and coffee tables,
strewn over rugs. I suggested she might want to put stick-

ers on lamp bases and check off paintings with me. I had always settled for white stickers and a simple numbering system. Livvy asked to stop at a stationery supply so she could color-code. Then, she said, she could apply the colors to a computer program I hadn't even heard about, which she downloaded and showed me how to operate. She would photograph everything with her digital camera. I bought her lots of cards and batteries and I gave her a gavel, the kind that could fit in the palm of her hand. I told her more about auction heat, the way you get sucked in.

I had just come out to sit by the pool, a lemonade in hand, as Livvy tucked her springy hair into a red swim cap. She wore a metallic cabana suit.

—Franny was a decent appraiser, I said.

Livvy pressed her dark, polarized goggles into place. I wasn't positive, but I thought she was looking at me. When she turned her head the light off her goggles blinded me momentarily.

—I know what you're thinking, she said.

I took one of Livvy's Oreos from a bowl and dunked it into my gin and tonic.

—You wish the train had hit you instead.

It took me a full minute, or what seemed like a full minute to say:

—No, that wouldn't . . .

—I would have jumped in front of the train to save her.

I tried to gauge exactly what we were talking about.

—But she'd want you alive and well, Livvy.

—I'm not copying her, you know. I just think it's cool that you can place a value on anything.

—I know, I said.

What I didn't say was that sometimes you feel none of it has any value. Even though you study the marks, signatures, stamps, provenance. Remove drawers from chests, turn chairs upside down, bracket objects in time.

I sucked on the cookie and stared into the center of her reflective suit, going through some revisionist thinking about the need to rescue others. Then she hit the water, finding a place that created almost no wake. I looked at the bits of chocolate and icing that floated in my drink. Livvy had learned the dolphin kick. Her stroke would overreach her mother's in time.

From the master suite you could see the lake through open silk curtains. If you hit a button, you could shut those blue panels and nap in unlimited thread count between shows. You could spread out a pizza box, movie catalogs, laptop, notes, and still have room for five people to sleep comfortably on the bed. You could make the television rise up out of the master-suite floor.

We brought movies to the estate. Watched *My Man Godfrey, To Be or Not to Be, Mr. and Mrs. Smith, In Name Only, Hands Across the Table, Nothing Sacred,* and *The Princess Comes Across.* Carole Lombard. I'd read that she had a mouth. Knew how to say words like: *shit* and *piss* and *fuck.* There was a mini-entertainment center in the bathroom. When Livvy went off to wander, I listened to Carole laugh and I soaked my head. I dried off and slipped into one of the cabana robes and imagined how differently she would have gone through the action of putting her arms into the sleeves.

A little Hepburn, Myrna Loy, Stanwyck before the hard edge took over, Claudette Colbert. But Lombard, she was it. While I cataloged, I considered her pacing. Her timing. The way the lighting brought out her cheekbones. I loved watching her bite into a piece of bread. Though she didn't eat a lot on screen, she knew how to make each mouthful work. I got a DVD of Academy Award ceremonies, and she was on that, so I saw how Lombard moved and comported herself during public events. But for all that watching, I couldn't define the *it* of Lombard. Her true value. Had no idea what she stayed up late to talk over with Gable. I wasn't able to hear the thoughts that fled through her mind when her plane went down. Even if sometimes I thought I knew what it was like for Gable when he got the news.

Livvy focused in the library, poring over the Edward Curtis collection. The Lewis Carroll photographs. I intercommed her to join me, or e-mailed her in the library to let her know about the new titles I had. She liked old movies okay, but not the way I did. Mike could watch for hours on end.

Livvy said something to me as we peeled the cellophane off our luncheon fruit plates in the formal dining room.

—You have to move on from Lombard.

I took the movies back and tried to clear my head. I picked up my wrappers and stayed out of the tub. I shifted to a little wine at night. I redoubled my efforts on the job and offered to pay Livvy for the time she had put in. But she wouldn't accept my money. Later I would discover she had taken a few things from the house. A couple of swimsuits, a paperweight, a cell from a Tweetie Bird cartoon. Nothing that added up to much.

twenty-five

Most evenings we got takeout, ran small errands. Once inside the downstairs door to my building, I sent Livvy ahead with the key while I collected the mail. The boxes were always stuffed with magazines. We were a real magazine culture in my building, and then I think some people never came home and their subscriptions stacked up.

By the time I got upstairs, Livvy would have her plate loaded with food. She liked to go off to my bedroom, shut the door, make calls, turn the music up, get on the Internet, while she watched a soundless TV. I think it was her way of mitigating life in general.

One night she left the bedroom door open, the entertainment shut down. No plate, no food. She sat on my bed, shoulders rounded, the only light in the room from the courtyard. I thought of an Edward Hopper painting.

—Can I get you something?

—No.

I leaned against the dresser by the door. There was the perfume bottle of Franny's that I had pocketed before leaving the West Coast.

—Sure?

—Taylor was just bullshitting me, you know. He said he was going to die if I didn't. Blah, blah, blah.

Livvy got up and turned on a sign. The room was hit by color and message. *Safe, Clean, Efficient.*

—A guy I kind of hung out with in college, named Stewart, he took that off a café called the Nuclear Reactor. That was my first neon. Stewart would have done anything for me. He'd be out in the living room right now if I hadn't broken up with him. We'd have nothing to say to each other, but he'd be nesting in my couch getting buzzed. And that kind of devotion isn't any better than . . . Start over, Mattie. There are two things I do about loss. I try to treat myself as Franny treated me. And when that doesn't work, because I'm too far gone, I notice how the *f*s in *Efficient* look like tiny switchblades. I watch the light that comes off the porch in search of the living room.

—I don't get it, she said.

—I don't either. But somehow it grounds me to remember the physical world.

—You want to watch a movie?

—Sure.

—*American Beauty?*

—I could watch *American Beauty.* Unless you want to see the Marx Brothers.

—Mom's going to stay at Franny's for a while. She's having a big fight with Aunt Nan about it.

Mike had sent me an e-mail that day. So it was no surprise when she told me Mona would be at her cousins' for a couple of weeks in Rhode Island, and he was coming to Chicago on Thursday to pick up Livvy.

—I guess we're going back to Boston and who knows.

Livvy warmed up the TV. Got the DVD out of the case.

—You think we should show him Lozenge World? I asked.

—Guess.

She sat cross-legged on the bed and moved through the scene selections.

—I saw a movie with Taylor and at the end they had a special feature and you could see all these dead soldiers. I wasn't sure if it was Iraq or some other war. But there were photos, like yearbook pictures, and it said their names and how old they were and where they came from and stuff.

I took a spot on the bed and pulled the comforter up.

—We'll go to an auction next time you're out. I'll line it up.

Livvy dug a handful of Kleenex out of the box and handed it to me.

—It's not like they're anyone we knew.

twenty-six

Some swimmers put a hard bend into their elbows and cut the water like a scythe, some appear to be slicing bread, but Livvy's summer coach had her doing a stroke with a full reach. It looked easy, uncomplicated. Not that I could mimic it. I watched her dolphin-kick off the end of the pool, how she turned her body to propel herself halfway down its length before surfacing again. Where I breathed on both sides, Livvy was a one-sided breather and passed the depth markers as if they were there to tick off distance and she had a fixed destination in mind. Sometimes I think that fluid addiction was the one thing that kept her going that summer.

When she stopped, she joined me in the whirlpool. Resting against the green tiles, we looked out at the flat action of the lake and skipped dumb reasons for talk. I had always been awkward about saying good-bye. Mike would arrive in an hour and Livvy, who had stayed up until three A.M., decided to take a nap before he got there. She would be in the library.

As she dripped into the house, I put on one of the

sarongs pressed and folded in the cabana. Then I did a mine-sweep of the entry hall and checked the security monitors, opened the gate by remote. I pinned up my wet hair and I set out lunch plates in one of the informal dining rooms, everything preordained by the catering service.

When the gravel finally popped in the drive, I launched over to a bank of windows and tried to run through the ten things I had planned to say, but each was like a fish swimming independently from its tank.

Mike pulled up in an orange-and-gray SUV, one of those things you can hose out after camping or windsurfing. He wore his beat-in leather jacket and a Harry Potter T-shirt. He looked weary and too handsome for my purposes. I slowed, breathed, and pulled the front doors open. He held me briefly, asked how I was, what Livvy was up to. I told him she was napping, and pointed to the house, as if he had X-ray vision and could see the library on the lake side.

—I'm sorry she can't stay longer.

He looked around as if the next thing to say had spilled on the drive, waiting to be picked up.

—Let's let her sleep a little, he said and told me they were driving to Boston, instead of flying. We discussed his route for a while. Then I asked him if I could gently pull his hair back to see the whole scar.

—Jesus.

—That's where they popped my old life out.

I asked if they had used factory parts, if he was in pain, how Mona was getting along, if he wanted a tour. He said she was happy to be with her cousins, and sure, he was into walking around, and there wasn't too much pain. He got a couple of things from the backseat and handed me a box. Inside was a hat Mona had made for me, using one of her craft kits. It looked like something for a doll or a small animal. Maybe it was intended to keep the contents of a head together, even if it couldn't quite meet the job. I hoped he didn't notice my hands shaking.

—And this, he said, and gave me a DVD.

—Franny's house, and there are a couple of minutes at the Miramar. The blue roofs before they go.

I wanted to feel detachment. I wanted to see the end as a coat I could put my arms into. But it was too hot out.

—You got my letters, didn't you?

I could almost see the light leaking from his seams.

—I read them in my sleep, I said, and explained about my current mode of sleepwalking.

—So . . . unconsciously you understand what I was trying to say?

It was the worst kind of avoidance, but I told him I just had to run in and leave a note for Livvy. I grabbed two bottles of water from the fridge and we walked the grounds, through the elms, over to the central garage. I opened one of the doors and while he looked around, I went over to the Maserati and reached under the dash and started to hot-wire.

—What are you doing?

—Addressing fear.

—I'm impressed.

I pulled the car out of the garage and opened the passenger-side door.

—Get in.

He did and I put the car into neutral and took my foot off the clutch, got the hand brake on. He tucked a strand of hair behind my right ear. I tried to let the current ease.

—We're going to sit here and idle while I tell you a story. About the time I was hit with 220 volts of electricity, I said.

—I don't remember that.

—It happened ten years ago at Shaver Lake, in California. At Camp Edison. No, it really did. It's a beautiful campground with good showers, a store. It even has a small laundry facility. I was there with a friend and we had her canoe, which we took out every day. She liked to go out even under large black clouds. A metal canoe on a lake in the hope of a storm. But the funny thing was, nothing happened when we were sitting ducks.

—I think that would be more than 220.

—Yes.

He put his hand on my right knee, and I took his hand and held it for a while.

—So you know those big industrial dryers in Laundromats? On the last day we packed up our gear, I decided to wash my hiking clothes and when I put the stuff in the dryer, it cut out on me. I didn't want to haul the wet clothes back to my friend's house because we had a day-and-a-half drive ahead. So I looked around and the back of the dryer was exposed on one side. And this small wire seemed to be out of place. I stood up in one of those laundry baskets, and I thought, for some inexplicable reason, that I could fix the dryer. When I put my hand on it . . .

—God, Mattie.

—It seemed like two minutes before I could pull away, though it probably wasn't. Later I talked to an electrician and he said they call that wire the disconnector. That he likes to stay clear of disconnectors. He said the reason I couldn't let go of the fucking disconnector was that it makes your muscles flex so your fingers tighten around the thing you want to release.

—Give it some time, he said.

—You have to get this. Even if you and Jane divorce . . .

—You should have read my letters.

—We'd always be triangulated.

—We'll hire a fucking electrician.

—Do you have any idea how much information exists on the miseries of triangulated relationships? It's all online and you can put it into your head faster than you can pour a glass of milk.

He reached into his jacket pocket and pulled out a notebook. He flipped through pages of scribbles, as if he were leafing through possible outcomes. When he stopped, he showed me a series of numbers he had written down.

—Here. Look. This is a reservation for the Plaza Hotel, for the Saturday after next. I got a great room overlooking the park. I'm offering you chaos, Mattie. You can't turn chaos down. I love you.

I was aware of swallowing so my eyes wouldn't run.

I shook my head, *No.*

He stared off, maybe two minutes. Then he got out, his hand still on the door. He was about to say something. But I pulled away, down the drive, and joined the light traffic heading north.

Downshifting, I went past those homes thick with arrival and Botticelli linen. I turned up the radio. They were talking about the growth of chaos, the index climbing. In that way my mind turns to pictures, I saw the linen closets of those mansions pop open like long-delayed flowers. White silk flew from the windows and chimneys of the estates along the lake. The fabric slipped into the air above Sheridan Road and caught for a moment on the windshield, then blew off as I got to the ravines. Lois once said: *A car will change your life.* But it wasn't about the Jaguar.

You go to the ravines when you want to pick up speed and maneuver turns. You drive right through a split in the earth and the air cools down and the light through the trees strobes your eyes. The estates and their nonsensical possessions up on the hills now. You can see peaks mostly, chimney tops, driveways.

The trees began to thin, the earth leveled out. I turned in at Ravinia. I had seen Jaco Pastoris there, Keith Jarrett, Nina Simone. The concert grounds were closed but I pulled into the drive and listened. I searched compartments for East Coast maps, hidden navigation systems. I popped the hood and checked the oil and water, windshield-wiper fluid, tire pressure. A little low. I could get air along the way.

I made one call. He was a little distracted, but my boss didn't seem to mind the idea of a short research trip.

The phone went in and out of reception, but I think he said: *more billable hours.*

I kept the business of the car to myself. A fucking beautiful machine.

afterword

The Miramar Hotel was demolished, but the investors, who planned a four-star resort, ditched the project. The 17-acre property sat for years, fenced off, unwaiting. I read the other day that it was acquired by a local billionaire. A tourist once asked me if John F. Kennedy and Jacqueline Bouvier stayed at the Miramar Hotel on their honeymoon. She had heard that the Kennedys fell in love with the blue roofs, walked Miramar Beach daily past Fernald Point. But she was getting hotels mixed up. They were up in the foothills at San Ysidro Ranch.

acknowledgments

My infinite gratitude to:
Sven Birkerts, Sandy Blau and Norton Kay, Christina Rago Brown, Melissa Chinchillo, Martha Cooley, Barry and Suzanne Cooperman, Emilia Dubicki, Shari Fineman, Christy Fletcher, Jennifer Freed, Jenny Lawton Grassl, Mark and Danielle Green, Sheridan Hay, Amy Hempel, Alice Kay, Jeff King, Rick Kogan, Sheila Kohler, Lyn Kustal, Margot Livesey, Jill McCorkle, Askold Melnyczuk, Joanna Meyer, Rick Moody, Kyoko Mori, Jinx Nolan and Bob Livermore, Pamela Painter, Fred Ramey, Liam Rector and the Bennington Writing Seminars, Judith Rosen, Elizabeth Searle, Caitlin Hamilton Summie, Kerry Tomlinson, Kate Scherler, Michael Steinberg, Lane Stewart, Mary Sullivan, Daniel Tobin, and all of my students.